The Soldier's Heart

Anthology

Allana Kephart ♥ Sam Destiny ♥ Bella Sterling
C.M. Lehsten ♥ Jamie Summer
Becky Elizabeth ♥ C.L. Foster ♥ E.R. Rada
Lissa Lynn Thomas ♥ Arielle Adams

This Soldier's Heart - 2018 © Copyright for each story is held, all rights reserved, by the individual author.

All rights reserved. No part of this publication may be reproduced, distributed, or transmitted in any form or by any means, or stored in a database or retrieval system, without the prior written permission of the authors.

This book is a work of fiction. Names, characters, places, and incidents are products of the author's imagination and/or are used fictitiously. Any resemblance to actual events, locales, or persons living or dead, is entirely coincidental.

The authors acknowledge the copyrighted or trademarked status and trademark owners of the word marks mentioned in this work.

This book is licensed for your personal enjoyment only. No part of this book may be reproduced in any form or transmitted by any electronic or mechanical means, including photocopying, information storage and retrieval systems, recording, or otherwise without the explicit written permission from the authors, except by a reviewer who may quote brief passages in a review.

If you would like to share the book with another person, please purchase an additional copy. Thank you for respecting the hard work of the authors.

For information on usage, contact Allana Kephart at: allanakephartauthor@gmail.com

Created and printed in the United States of America.
First Edition February 2018
ISBN-10: 1984090690
ISBN-13: 978-1984090690

♥

Cover Design by Emma Rider at Moonstruck Cover Design

Interior design and typesetting by Christy Foster of Phoenix Quill Formatting

Editing by Allana Kephart

Anthology
Table of Contents

Dedication 5
Forward
   A.L. Shea 7
Be Mine, Valentine
   Becky Elizabeth 9
Beautiful Trauma
   Allana Kephart 11
A Tagged Valentine
   Sam Destiny 35
This Soldier's Heart
   Bella Sterling 55
A Soldier's Enchantment
   C.M. Lehsten 57
Never Knew Goodbye
   Jamie Summer 83
Restless
   Arielle Adams 127
A Soldier's Sunset
   C.L. Foster & E.R. Rada 129
Shut Up and Kiss Me
   Lissa Lynn Thomas 159

About The Authors

    Becky Elizabeth 177

    Allana Kephart 179

    Sam Destiny 181

    Bella Sterling 183

    C.M. Lehsten 185

    Jamie Summer 187

    Arielle Adams 189

    C.L. Foster 191

    E.R. Rada 193

    Lissa Lynn Thomas 195

Dedication

For all the lost souls, hopeless dreamers, broken-hearted, war-torn heroes, and those who still believe in love.

And to our brave soldiers, near and far.
Thank you for your service.

This Soldier's Heart

Forward
A.L. Shea

Love is a strange and wonderful thing. There are all kinds of love in the world, from romantic, to familial, and so many variations in between. Love is the great equalizer. It sets us all on the same level. It has the power to raze us to the ground. But it also has the power to heal; to lift us up and fill us with joy.

The service men, women, and people who put their lives on the line to serve their countries, do this out of love; love of family, of country, of freedom. We salute them and pay tribute to their bravery and sacrifice here with these stories of love, loss and romance. All proceeds from the sale of this volume will be donated to a charity that benefits those brave men, women, and people.

On Valentine's Day, we celebrate love in all its forms, and invite you to join us and do the same.

This Soldier's Heart

Be Mine, Valentine
Becky Elizabeth

My armour
chipped away
gaping holes
give way to the knives
in my back

but I stand proud
with my once beaten heart
aglow with the truth of this

my love is the sword in my hands

and I'd die for you.

I'd kill
for you.

This love is all I'll ever need
to survive the battles of time;

This Soldier's Heart

it is protected
your life,
for mine.

Because now my once tattered heart beats steady

it resides in your chest
while I remain guardian
over every delicate piece of yours.

Two warriors
intertwined

making a mockery
of the battlefield
of the memories
strewn out like fallen corpses

the past that shaped us
into what we are today.

Together
we are unbreakable.

Beautiful Trauma
Part I
Allana Kephart

Prologue
Bridgette

Crickets chirp in the darkness, singing their ballad of woe into the dank night air. My black dress is soaked at the knees, the evening dew on the grass seeping in and staining the crushed velvet. I can't bring myself to care—the moisture isn't what chills my bones tonight. The folded-up flag on my lap carries the weight of the world, crushing me under the reality of it all.

In Memory of Brett Daniels
MAA
U.S. Navy
Beloved Brother & Son
30 November 1985
14 February 2015

I stare at the tombstone, the one so much like our father's and I wonder, bitterly, how I could have prevented this. What I could have done differently that might have brought Brett off this ledge. I hugged him every single night, I told him I loved him as much as one could stand without being a creep. I thought I did everything right—but clearly, I missed the signs.

Keep it together, Bridgette, I tell myself. *Brett would never forgive himself for making you cry.*

My older brother Brett was a decorated U.S. Navy veteran. He spent six years of his too short life serving our country only to come back and take his own life a year later. No one suspected a thing. We'd hear him wandering around in the middle of the night, and he couldn't hold a job, but we chalked it up to 'readjustments' and moved on with our lives.

And now Brett would never move on with his. . .

"Bridgette," my mom's voice comes from behind me. The funeral service ended hours ago, but I couldn't move my feet to attend Brett's reception. Mom let me stay here and promised she'd come pick me up, but when I remained as cold as a statue even then, she just sat down next to me and waited. That was almost three hours ago. "It's nearly midnight."

I stay quiet.

"We should head home," she prods gently. "You need some rest."

How could I rest? I could still see him when I closed my eyes, hanging in the closet from the belt I bought him for Christmas only two months ago, his face swollen and purple, wide brown eyes dull and lifeless. If I did fall asleep, Dad's laugh haunted me in my dreams, the night he left for his tour in Vietnam and came back in a body bag. And in wake, my mother lay alone in the next room, choking on bile as the chemo wreaked havoc on her failing body. I could listen to her hack and wonder what will happen to her if I'm the next body in our family—if the path I took after my fallen father and brother toward defending my country would leave the strongest woman I've ever known alone.

Peace was nowhere to be found—how could she expect I'd get any rest ever again?

I shake my head and she sighs, her frail arms wrapping around my shoulders and pulling me against her chest. "I know it's hard, Gette. But it's going to be okay—the world moves on."

"I don't want it to," I say, my voice pitchy from tears. "I don't want the world to go on without Brett, without Daddy."

Mom kisses my hair. "Me neither," she admits. "But you know what? Brett and Daddy loved us more than anything in this world. And true love never really dies, Gette."

I nod, though her sentiment is lost on me.

I wish I could believe her.

Chapter I
Bridgette

Whiskey blurs my vision so thoroughly I can hardly see Sidney Prescott's white cotton bra before she's tackled to the bed by a boy I've never understood the appeal towards, while the gang of drunken idiots discuss basic How to Die in a Horror Flick 101 downstairs. This is only the seven-hundred and thirty-second time I've watched this movie in my life—normally, it's my absolute favorite. The ridiculousness of the movie has always raised my spirits even in my darkest moments, but it's just not doing the trick for me tonight.

It's Valentine's Day. A day for cheap chocolate and red roses, for love letters and unbridled passion. For me, it's a twisted reminder of how alone a person can truly be. My brother hung himself on this day almost half a decade ago, on the anniversary of our father's funeral, and last year, my mother lost her battle to cancer in the predawn Hallmark Holiday light.

That's the last of my family. If I remember correctly, my dad's little sister, Aunt Nikki, lives somewhere in Bumfuck Nowhere, South Dakota, but I haven't seen her since pre-puberty, when I told Dad I was going to be just like him when I grew up and join the army and Aunt Nikki about choked on her tea.

"*The army!*" *she'd gasped.* "Bridgette, that is no *place for a lady!*"

I love what I do. But sometimes I think I should have listened to her. I'd probably have fewer handfuls of nightmares to drown.

Two more years on my current tour, and I'll probably sign up for another six once I'm done. Two tours down, what's one more, right? It's not like I have anything waiting for me here in the states.

I startle out of my thoughts when people start screaming in the movie and I rub the sleep out of my eyes. It's barely ten P.M., that's too early for even me to go to sleep. Not while I'm on vacation, I think the fuck not. No 0600 wake up calls here—no need to waste the buzz I've worked so hard to achieve.

Hauling myself off the couch with tremendous effort, I rush to the bathroom to take account of my appearance. A brush of mascara, a tint of blush, and a swipe of cherry red lip gloss is all the effort I'm willing to put in for the evening. My hair is a wild mess on my head, my eyes tired, but I don't care. I will be normal tonight.

Rifling through the boxes of clothes I moved here from my mom's house after her death, I find a slip of a dress and squeeze into it. I've had it since senior prom—a ruched emerald dress with sequins down the front—and I remember back then, it didn't fit. I was curvier then, filled out in all the right places. Now, stress and overexertion has destroyed my hourglass figure and it hangs limply over my hips.

I brush my hair out of my eyes and frown at the mirror. I don't recognize the girl in front of me, the eyes so heavy with trauma, the wear and tear on my young bones.

I'm starting to understand why Brett did what he did. There's nothing I could have done to save him.

Whatever.

I'm not going to worry about anything like the service, my family, or my mental state tonight. Tonight, I'm taking my tipsy ass downtown to have a good time.

Just like a normal civilian.

Chapter II

Henry

Writing poetry with intent, I'd say, is the easiest way to self-induce a migraine from hell. Back when I let myself write freely, as a nobody living in my beat-up old Chevy, the words came as if written by another through my hands.

And then, I got an agent.

I went on tours, bared my naked soul to crowds of judgmental eyes until I felt raw from exposure, signed books filled with words I always felt were inadequate and yet, in spite of all that, couldn't find any publisher to sign me. I blew through my savings and destroyed myself chasing after a dream I didn't achieve. My agent insists it's the content of my poems—the market is saturated with mental health and struggles of being alone, and people don't want to hear more sad stories when their lives are miserable enough as is.

"More 'heart eyes', less 'sad face'," he says. "Okay, Hen?"

Where he wants me to pull inspiration for these 'heart eyes' poems escape me. I have as much luck with women as a dead goldfish would have climbing a tree. I can't pinpoint what exactly is so appalling about me—I have heard from 'helpful' prospects that I'm too kind, too artistic, too me. I don't know how to change that, so I have resigned myself to a lonely death.

Apparently, that doesn't bode well for publishing companies.

I slam my laptop closed and drop my head against the cold surface. The muse is dead tonight and I am in no mood to beat a dead horse. It's Valentine's day, and I'm sober. That's gotta be illegal in one of the countries on this planet, right?

The problem is, I am flat broke. Being a starving artist will do that to you. Which means I have no liquor in this house. The only way I'll be getting drunk tonight is to go to the bar.

"Now, I know what you're thinking," I say aloud to the empty air. "How are you gonna get drunk at a bar when you have no money, bars cost more money than bottles! Well, I'll tell you, you pompous figment of my imagination. People abandon their drinks all the time! That's how."

I shake my head at myself. I'm losing it. It's official. I need social interaction, before I start seeing things.

Time for a night on the town!

But first. . . shower.

Chapter III
Bridgette

The hallway was drafty and smelled like dust, making me long for the post outside where one could watch the stars and smell the fresh cut grass. It was week 5 of Basic Combat Training, and I was put on guard duty, third shift. Nearly 3 in the morning now, but I didn't mind. I was elated to be moving up in rank, for my superiors to trust me with this task.

"How ya holdin' up, Daniels?" he asked, breezing around the corner in his dark blue uniform. Commander Stroh had been with the military for nearly two full decades, sacrificed everything for the sake of his country. At the time, I couldn't even imagine the horrors he'd witnessed.

"I'm fantastic!" I chirped. He raised a brow at me, his mouth curled in an amused smirk and I scrambled to say, "Er—sir. I'm fantastic, sir."

"Glad to hear it," he chuckled. "Bootcamp isn't for everybody, you know."

"I assure you I'm up to the challenge," I said brightly. "Sir."

With a sweet grin he stepped closer, into my space, I could smell the sweat of his last training. "You've been quite... impressive, to me, over the last few weeks, Bridgette."

The use of my first name caught me off guard and I straightened, pressing my lips together in uncertainty. "Thank you, sir," I said.

His hand reached for me, clutching a fistful of my jacket and he pulled me off my feet. I stumbled into him, clapping my palms against his T-shirt clad chest and tried to push back, but he held strong. "Sir, what—"

"You'll be enduring your hardest task tomorrow," he said calmly, as though I wasn't doing my damnedest to shove him away. "A lot of people get lost."

Stroh flipped me around suddenly, forcing my face against the concrete wall of the hallway as he fitted his body against mine. His arm was pinned over my shoulders as his hips rolled into me, and I felt the length of him fit into the curve of my ass.

"Get off me," I snarled, hating myself for the way my voice shook.

"You wouldn't want to get lost, now, would you, Private?"

I haul off and land my fist into the delicate face behind my shoulder. Blood pools from his nose as a sickening thwack! reverberates down my forearm and into my chest. Without hesitation, I swing my knee up and land it solidly between the man's legs, watching him crumple to the ground with a sick twist of satisfaction.

"Pig!" I spit.

"Yo, what the fuck?!" A man screams from behind me. He rushes to his collapsed friend, piercing me with a dark-eyed glare. "Crazy bitch."

I blink the haze out of my eyes, the situation I'm in coming back into focus. I'm not in that dusty hallway on base—I'm on the rooftop of a crowded bar, packed in between sweaty, drunken bodies. And the man I just attacked wasn't Commander Stroh, but some innocent civilian who got a little too handsy with me when I didn't want to dance.

Panic overtakes me again, but with new reasoning. *I punched a civilian.*

"I-I'm s-so sorry," I stutter, but it goes unheard. The bass is too loud to hear what anyone says if they're not screaming. A small crowd forms around the fallen man, other creeps smirking at my ferocity and I sprint to the exit before the blackout really takes over.

The cold air hits my cheeks, freezing the tears in my eyes before they can fall, and I don't stop running until my legs quiver and I fall to my knees on the pavement.

Stupid, stupid, stupid! What the hell was I thinking? This is real life, the life I have to return to one day. And I couldn't handle a little dirty dancing between intoxicated strangers? How was I ever going to come back to the real world when my mind did this to me at the drop of the hat, when the nightmares followed me even in wake?

"Hey!" someone yells, but I don't turn to see. It's only when his boots come into my view that I realize he's talking to me. "Miss? Are you alright?"

"Don't touch me," I snap, though he wasn't trying to.

He kneels down in front of me, palms out in surrender. "Are you alright?" he asks again.

"Who's asking?" I bite.

He holds his hand closer to me. I hope he didn't see me flinch. "Henry Hall," he says. "I saw what happened back there. He was way outta line." He pauses, his dark brows knitting together when he says, "Granted, you may have overreacted, but he was being a perv, so."

I narrow my eyes at him until he drops his hands back in his lap, swelling with misplaced pride at the confusion on his face. "I'm just fine," I say.

"Cool, cool," he rattles nervously. He cracks his knuckles against themselves, brown eyes wide like a lost puppy. "You, uh. You're bleeding."

"What?" I ask, surveying myself. My knees are scraped and cut to ribbons, pebbles and glass shards stuck in the skin. I curse obnoxiously, wiping the sweat off my forehead with the back of my hand. "Fuck me."

"Please, miss," dude says. "I haven't even bought you a drink."

"Ha, ha, you're hilarious." I rise to my feet and wobble, the world tipping as I try to stand. It would appear I'm more drunk than I thought.

Dude—what was his name again?—reaches for me, his hands soft against my frigid elbows. "Easy now," he says gently. "Can you walk?"

I try to cuss him out, but I can't even understand myself when I talk. His brow knits together again, and I snort at the sight. "Stupid," I mutter.

"Thank you," he says, but his lips curl up at the corners.

"Laughin' phat meh?" I slur. He chuckles outright, but doesn't answer. Prick.

"C'mon. Let's get you home. Can you tell me where you live?"

"Stalker!" I shout in his face. "Why would—who'dyou think you are, buddy?"

He sighs and snags my purse off my arm. I'm disgusted by the lack of effort I put into getting it back. He plucks my ID from its home in my wallet and nods to himself. "Well, Bridgette, you're in luck. I know where this is. My agent lives right around there."

Something about the way my name rolls off his tongue makes me feel molten inside. That's new. I want to ask him to say it again—maybe slower, whispered in my ear. "Agent?" I ask instead.

He grins. "Wouldn't you like to know? Now shush. If you throw up on me, I'm gonna be very upset."

I rub my eyes, damning the tequila for dominating my libido like this. I vaguely remember cursing at a few people who passed us by for judging me, and a police officer asking if we were alright before we made it to my house.

Dude took my purse again to fetch my keys. I blacked out after that.

Chapter IV
Henry

Benefit #1 of having no friends, family, or social life: I never have to babysit drunks.

I had completely forgotten just how difficult it could be to drag a stumbling adult along after you for two whole blocks. This feisty creature, Bridgette Daniels, was a whole new level of fucked up. Her knees wobble with every step, and tears pour down her face, but I don't think she really notices. She's too busy asking me why I'm so obsessed with her, and part of me wishes I was the type of sleaze to leave a girl behind a dumpster for the evening. Lord knows it would have made my night less eventful.

"Bridgette," I say, biting back a laugh at the sneer she sends me. "Keys—I need your keys."

She sniffs at me, crossing her arms and looking away from her front door. I huff at her for the millionth time that night and steal her bag once more. The sudden shock to her side tips her center of gravity, and with a squeal, she falls against my chest.

I brace myself for the punch, but she surprises me by burying her face in my neck and giggling like a fiend. I'm momentarily distracted by how well she fits against me, how right it feels to have her in my arms, before I shake myself out of it. Damn artistic brain, making every inconvenience romantic.

"Alright, Bridge, take it easy," I say, unlocking her door and guiding her inside. It's practically barren—two black couches and a mahogany coffee table in front of a small television, no rugs, blankets, or pillows to be found. It's freakishly clean, not even a speck of dust on the mantel, where the only evidence of life is found—two folded flags, beside a silver urn.

Questions bubble up in my throat, but I swallow them down. This girl couldn't tell me if we were in the right house if her life depended on it, let alone explain the emptiness of it all.

"Creepy," she murmurs at me, glaring up into my eyes.

"Mhmm. Can you show me to your room?"

"Why?" she asks. "You gonna follow me?"

"To the end of the world, Bridgette," I reply sarcastically.

She pauses, her head tilting at the joke. "Cute. That'd make me feel so much better about myself."

I'm taken aback by the hatred in her voice, the heavy weight of disgust at the thought of someone following her, of all people. "Is that so?" I ask.

"Oh yes." She smiles. "So much better."

Man, I wish she was sober. I want to know more about her. . .

"Bedroom!" She declares around a yawn. I need to push my curiosity aside and put the drunkard to bed.

Her bedroom is much like the rest of her house—sterile. Cardboard boxes spill free of an otherwise empty closet, her bed is made perfectly—military style.

That would explain the flags.

Bridgette releases a pleased sound and rips herself from my embrace, flinging herself onto the bed. Her bloodied knees smear into the perfect white sheets and I cringe, gently rolling her onto her back. "Can I help you clean up?"

She's out cold.

I rub my temples and retreat to the bathroom, finding a first aid kit beside three yellow towels in the cupboard. It's the only fleck of color I've seen in this whole house—I wonder if yellow is her favorite color, or if they were on sale.

Why do I care? It's not like I'll ever see this girl again.

I clean up her knees best I can and wrap them in gauze, before leaving two ibuprofen and a glass of ice on her nightstand. By morning, the ice will melt, and she'll have crisp water to soothe what will be a horrible hangover. Last minute, I push her trash bin beside her head on the floor.

Not like I've done this before.

My intentions were to leave immediately after that. I swear. But another splotch of color caught my eye as I opened the door—a dark blue bottle of vodka.

I'm not desperate enough to steal her liquor... But a glass or two as payment for practically saving her life couldn't hurt.

Right?

Chapter V
Bridgette

It's not my internal clock that wakes me up this morning. No men screaming to get my ass in gear, no nightmares shocking me back to reality. No. This morning? It's the inarguable fact that someone has a chainsaw to the back of my head.

A moan of agony pours from my throat, and the sound blasts back in my head. My stomach revolts, rejecting the poison I ingested last night, and I roll over, vomiting the entirety of my stomach contents into the trash can.

Oh God, I will never drink again, I think, afraid of my own voice. This is a fate worse than death, surely.

I puke until I heave, until my ribs hurt from the strain, and then wonder where the trashcan came from. I know I didn't put it there—I have no recollection of the night before, but I damn sure wasn't thinking clear enough to prep for the onslaught of illness this morning.

I catch sight of the chilly water and headache meds beside me and I snatch them up like gold, swallowing the whole of them in one gulp. The cool water caresses my burned throat and cuts through the acid churning in my stomach.

"Someone shoot me," I mutter, wracking my brain. There was a dude last night, wasn't there? Some random guy with chocolate brown eyes and curly, dirty blonde hair. He smelled like cinnamon and cayenne, spicy and hot and dangerous, but everything about him screamed angel boy.

Nah. Can't be. He's too perfect to exist—clearly a case of beer goggles.

Making my way down the stairs is harder than anything the army has put me through. And the army has broken me down to nothing before, so that's really saying something. I've never been this hungover in my life, and I intend to never be this fucked up again. I mean—damn. I'm screwed up enough to be imagining Dream Dude passed out on my couch right now.

...

Wait.

"What the fuck is this?" I hiss.

Dream guy groans into the crease between the back and the seat of my leather couch. I edge closer, stabbing my finger into his lower back, smirking when he growls at me like an angry pup. "Go'way. I'm dying."

"Not on my couch," I say with as much venom as I can muster without puking again.

"*Your* couch?" Dream guy pushes himself up slowly, his arm trembling with the effort. He rubs his eyes, blinking as he looks around my house. Blood rushes up his neck into his face, painting him less-than-appealing shade of crimson. "Oh no," he rasps, sitting up shakily. "Ah, shit, I—this is not what I wanted to do, I swear."

I chuckle. "What's your name again?"

He blinks at me, rubbing his eyes. "Henry."

"Henry," I murmur. I'll remember that. "Did we have sex last night, Henry?"

He jerks back like I struck him. "What? Oh, God, no, I would never—what kind of—of course we didn't have sex!"

"Hm." I sigh. "That's unfortunate."

I walk away as Dream Dude, Henry, sputters an attempt at a response. I smile to myself as I text in my usual Chinese order from the poor bastards at the corner shops. They surely rue the days I'm home from tour. I double my hangover order and return back to Henry with a new glass of water. "Lean your head back, and sit quietly. Food is coming."

I hear his jaw working as he tries to make himself speak, but eventually he gives in and closes his eyes.

For some reason, I'm not in the least bit uncomfortable with a stranger sitting on my couch. Who knows—maybe if my headache ebbs, we can remedy the missed opportunity of seeing each other naked.

Chapter VI
Henry

Bridgette and I clicked over hangovers and pot stickers. She's in the army, and I only have a week left with her before she has to go back overseas for another two years. Luckily, she gets time off back home. Only knowing her a week, I know she's worth the wait.

She's rugged, all sharp edges and mistrust, but something about her. . . I can't put my finger on it, but she's special. Brave. Resilient. I know she's holding back, keeping secrets from me, but I don't mind the wait. I've never felt like this before in my whole life.

Writing comes easier now—those sappy poems my agent has been dogging me for flow like water from a faucet. But I won't share them with anyone but her. Not now, not yet. Maybe if she rejects me after this attempt to show I'm interested in more than just friendship with her, then I'll blow them off and share them with the world.

For now, I'll settle for baring my soul in the form of love notes on paper towels.

Over the top? Maybe. But that's art, right?

I slip the paper towel in her open palm while she sleeps before dashing out the door. We haven't been apart since she found me on her couch four nights earlier, and it's about time I wash my own clothes and return the giant 'sleep shirts' she loaned me.

At least, that's what I tell myself.

In reality, I'm too afraid she won't feel the same.

Chapter VII
Bridgette

There was something unnerving
in the way you said if I followed you
just down the road
or the end of the Earth
how it would make you feel

"So much better"
about your beautiful self
as if you don't know you're worthy
of someone who sees the light in you

Do you shroud yourself
in darkness like I do?
Is your heart heavy
with a pain so unbearable
you're ashamed, too?

I wonder what scars you have
and if I'll ever have the privilege
of kissing them away
until you see yourself
like I do

I spend at least two hours reading and rereading the tender words written out on the paper towel. No one has ever done something like this for me—a poem? He sees right through me, the darkness in my heart that I can't quite shake, the scars I try so hard to hide. I could feel it when he looked at me. It felt like a physical touch when he stared into my eyes like they held the whole universe.

I'd never felt beautiful before he looked at me like that.

I sigh quietly, biting my lip as I read over the declaration another time. I wonder, idly, if the man with a soul so beautiful could feel so deeply about someone as tainted as me. It's like he feels I'm the light of his life, the angel he stumbled upon.

If he knew the truth about me, I know he'd run. And who could blame him?

I didn't realize just how. . . uninhabited my condo felt until I invited someone over. My bookshelves are empty, pictures in boxes shoved under the bed. I never went out of my way to make my mark here. After all, what if I were to die? Who would be left to clean up?

I remember packing up my brother's belongings, going through his darkest secrets and sorting them like library books. It felt so intrusive, prying into every drawer, every hiding place just to shove his things away. At least this way, if I'm killed, everything is packed up and ready for storage already.

I can hurt the ones I love less this way; by failing to exist.

What could I start here, inviting Henry in? Sure, he's interested in me. But how can that really be true? We've only just met. If I were to disappear, his life would move on, just like my mother once told me.

Anything could happen in a war—I could invite him into my heart just to potentially die half a world away? I could feed him this illusion of hope when I wouldn't eat the lie myself?

Was that fair?

My phone rings and breaks me out of my stupor, making me jump in surprise. "Henry?" I answer. The hope in my voice is embarrassing, but I want to hear his voice— I want to talk to him, after finding out how he feels.

"Think again, Daniels," Commander Stroh's voice comes over the phone, my blood running cold. "We need you back on base. Immediately."

"Commander, what—? What are you talking about, my leave isn't over ye—"

"I know, soldier, I'm sorry for that. But this is an urgent matter, life and death. You'll be briefed on the plane, there's no time for it now."

"But, sir—"

"Is there a *problem*, Daniels?" Stroh barks.

You wouldn't want to get lost. . .

I shiver, closing my eyes against the bile rising in my throat. I can't argue—if I give them any reason not to increase my rank, I'll be stuck working with this monster for the rest of my career. I can't let that happen.

"No, sir."

"I want you on the first flight out tonight. Your tickets will be waiting for you at the airport."

"Sir—" I hear his gruff, muffled growl and I bite my tongue. "Yes, sir."

Stroh hangs up without another word. I drop my phone on the bed, closing my eyes against the pain, the disappointment clawing at my throat.

This is for the best, I think. *For both of us.*

Henry will be back any minute, I'm sure of it. If I don't reach out to him, he'll come to see what I think of his letter.

If I move fast, I'll get out of here before he returns.

Chapter VIII
Henry

Bridgette's complex is far prettier than any place I've ever lived. The shrubs are tended, the grass is bright green and trimmed to the standard of a major league baseball field. Each window is pristine, and the paint job looks no older than six months. I almost feel like I don't belong, even knowing this isn't a wealthy neighborhood. Street bums don't belong around here. . .

I shake off my nerves and take a steadying breath, clutching my chest as I approach the door. She's in there—this girl I can see myself falling in love with, she's in there with my heart at her mercy. She knows what I want now. I have to know what she wants of me.

The door swings open as I raise my fist to knock, and Bridgette freezes in front of me, a duffle bag hangs off her slender shoulder, her face devoid of color and hidden beneath her camouflage hat. She's dressed for battle, in full army uniform, with papers in her hand like she's running away. "Henry," she whispers.

"What's this?" I ask. "Are. . . are you leaving?"

She swallows. "M-My commander called, demanded I come back early. My flight leaves in two hours."

"So, what, you were just gonna run off? Not call me at all?"

"Basically, yeah." The hurt must show on my face, because she steps closer and takes my hand in hers. "It's better this way, Henry. I hardly know you, you hardly know me—this is a blessing in disguise, somehow."

"How is this a blessing?" I demand. "How is cutting us short a blessing to you?"

She flinches, her eyes darkening at the implication she doesn't care. "I can't hurt you if I go now."

I shake my head. "Wanna bet?"

She lets out a low breath and looks away from me. "Goodbye, Henry."

She pushes past me, her hand over her mouth as she tries to duck into her car before I can stop her. I stop the front door before it slams shut, yelling after her, "I'll wait."

She stumbles to a halt, shoulders rigid.

"It's what? Two more years?" I ask, following her to the car. "That's what you said, right? That's nothing, Bridge—"

"Are you out of your fucking mind?" She turns to me, tears in her eyes and mouth agape.

"Quite possibly," I admit. "I don't care. I want to give us a chance to become something more than this—if it's now, or next week, or two years from now, it's okay. I'll wait for you."

"For how long?" she demands. "Huh? How long are you gonna wait for someone you don't even know?"

"However long it takes," I tell her truthfully. "I might hardly know you, but it doesn't feel that way. I feel like I've known you my whole life. I write for a living and I don't have the words to explain how I really feel about you, but I'm not running away from it. Not now, possibly not ever. Can't you give us a chance?"

"How could you ask me to leave you waiting here when you don't know who's going to come back?" she cries. "Hell, *if* I'll come back!"

My heart drops at the thought. "Is that what you're afraid of? Dying?"

She shakes her head. "No," she whimpers.

"Then what is it, Bridge?" I ask. "Why are you so afraid of having someone here waiting for you to come home?"

"I..." she lets out a low sigh. "I'm afraid of dying, and leaving you behind. I'm afraid of the hurt I'll blow into the world by being selfish and. . . and being *happy*."

Her body shivers with the sobs trying to break free, and I reach for her slowly, pulling her trembling body against mine. "So, what if you do?" I ask. "Any time with you, no matter how short, would be better to me than nothing at all."

She pulls in a quiet gasp, resting her head against my chest. "Your poem. . ."

I swallow past the lump in my throat. "What about it?" I prompt when she doesn't continue.

She looks at me, at a loss for words. Her mouth opens and closes several times, but no words come out. She huffs, her hands coming up to tangle in my hair and pull my mouth down to hers. And then she kisses me, her lips making promises I can only hope her heart will keep, and suddenly, in my soul I know everything she wanted to say.

A Tagged Valentine
A Tagged Soldiers Short Story
Sam Destiny

One

Corporal Jesse 'Jazz' Connor rang the doorbell, hardly able to see anything behind the dozen roses he'd bought for Tessa.

It was their first Valentine's together and as much as he loved her every damn day since he'd gotten her back—and tried to prove she was right in not having given up on him—he still wanted to do something special for her that day.

She laughed after opening the door, and the sound went straight to his heart, sending it racing—and chasing away a small part of what had him itching to run.

"You live here. You don't need to ring the doorbell. It's our home, Jazz," she stated and leaned around the flowers to kiss him.

Only after she'd taken the roses from him and turned to bring them inside did he take her in. She wore black heels underneath bootcut jeans, and a black long-sleeved top that left her shoulder and neckline free since she'd pulled her blonde hair into a ponytail.

God, she was beautiful, and she was his—and soon would be his wife, too. Luckily.

"When I said dress pretty I didn't think you'd be trying to drive me crazy," he muttered, and she finished arranging the flowers in a vase before turning to him, her dark eyes soft and warm.

"I didn't. I dressed rather casual, but you look mighty fine, my soldier." She crossed over to him and grabbed the lapel of his suit jacket. He was wearing dark jeans, but had combined it with a white button down and the jacket because he loved the way she looked at him then.

"You're always driving me crazy in the best way possible," he whispered and then leaned in to kiss the side of her neck where it met her shoulder.

Fuck, maybe they should just skip lunch and go straight to the rest of the evening.

"Was Ela okay with taking Johnny?" Of course she'd been. His mother had agreed about a million times, yet Jazz found it hard sometimes to let his son go—and accept that others were good with taking care of him, too.

Funny how some things changed with time, especially when he thought back to the beginning with his little boy.

Shaking the dark thoughts off, he wrapped his arms around Tessa, surprised by the intensity with which he feared losing her.

"I love you, and because I do, I brought you something."

She cocked her head. "You a mean a dozen roses? Because I saw that, and I love them."

Of course she did. The wine-red ones were her favorite—but only coming from him. She'd said that at some point, and he'd stuck to that.

"Yes, but no. Something else."

Stepping back, she placed her hands on her hips. "You're here. That's *all* I need."

Jesus, they were the cheesiest couple ever, and he didn't mind the slightest bit. Tessa was his life, and always would be.

He cupped the back of her neck and drew her in, kissing her sweet and slow. She tasted of raspberries and peaches, and he knew it was her new favorite Chapstick. The thought made him smile and she squinted at him.

"What's funny, handsome?"

Jazz shook his head. "Nothing, just... there's something calming in knowing a person's ins and outs. Something akin to pleasure in knowing everything about you. It puts my mind at ease."

Her expression got tender and she framed his face, brushing her thumb across his cheeks. "Aren't you just the weirdest kind of serious today? I already agreed to marry you. You can smile again. And beam. And laugh."

"Not serious, reflective. Anyway, wanna know what I have for you?"

Of course she did. He could read the curiosity in her eyes. "Fine, tell me."

He pulled out the necklace he'd gotten made for her and she clasped her hands in front of her mouth. It was silver, and the trinkets were a smaller version of dog tags with his and Johnny's name on one each. They were elegant and pretty, perfect for the woman who'd own them.

"Jesus, Jesse, what in the world...?" Tears were in her eyes as she carefully fingered the jewelry, her fingertips trembling against the silver. "God, it's perfect."

He smiled. "Just like you then. May I?" He nodded toward her neck and she turned, letting him put the necklace where it belonged.

When she faced him again, his gaze rested on the necklace, then he lowered his eyes, hiding them from her, worrying what she could read in them. How had he ever thought he'd be able to live his life for the army when this, life with Tessa, was everything a man should strive to achieve?

♥

Tessa soon-to-be Connor studied her fiancé's face, reaching out to cup his cheek again. "Jesse, I already told I'm all yours. You can stop being so nervous."

He'd gone all out with his proposal and although for the slightest moment she'd thought he was going to break up with her, the evening had ended in utter happiness. Now there were merely months left until they stood next to each other, and would become husband and wife.

She was dying for that day already. However, his mood had her worried.

"I know, but can I not still want to do something great for the woman I love? Would you please just kiss me as a thank you and stop making me worry even more?" he fussed, and she realized what was going on.

That day, of all days, the darkness was back. Taking his hand, she led him over to the sofa and pushed him onto it.

"Tess," he whispered, but she just crawled up on his lap, framing his face and kissing him until he sighed into her mouth, opening his lips for her, allowing her entrance.

He tasted of mint and uniquely of Jazz.

His arms wrapped around her, his fingertips digging into her sides, and she didn't mind because it meant he was there, with her.

Only when his shoulders sagged a little did she break the kiss, pulling away and leaving them panting.

"A flashback? Nightmare you didn't tell me about?" she asked quietly, roaming his face with her eyes, brushing through his dark hair.

"Hey, you're messing up my out-of-bed-look," he complained, and she laughed, mussing it again.

"There," she muttered, and he grinned.

"It's neither. Not a flashback. Not a dream. It's more... this restlessness inside of me, the feeling that you'd be torn from my side any second if I don't touch you. I..." He shook his head and she rubbed the tip of her nose alongside his jaw, kissing the pulsing vein on his neck, feeling the blood rush faster through it the longer she teased him.

"God, Tessa, you know what I wish we could do? Sleep under the stars by the beach. Our beach. And by sleep, I mean..." He wiggled his brows and she blushed, but grinned nonetheless. She liked that idea.

She liked that idea a whole lot. John would be okay with his grandma, and they had arranged for the day to be theirs. It was lunch time now and her stomach reminded her of that with a distinct growl.

"Oh God, I wanted to take you to lunch and you distracted me. Let's go, now."

She stood before he shoved her off in his hurry to rectify her hunger, and she shook her head.

"Let's take blankets," she suggested, and he paused by the door.

"I have some in the truck."

Tessa nodded in agreement, already making her way to the hallway closet. "I know, but let's take more."

She loved that they'd take the truck. She could've worn a gown and still would've preferred Jazz's baby to all other cars because it was theirs. It was just as much connected to their history as the beach or the airport.

She grabbed as many blankets as she could find, and joined Jesse in the living room again. He arched a brow, but didn't comment as she pointed him to take the two blankets from the back of the couch, following her as she dumped them all in the backseat.

"Do I want to know?" he asked as she slipped into the passenger side, leaning over to kiss him.

"Do you want to know what?" she asked innocently. He might have gone crazy planning this day, but she had a tendency to screw his plans anyway, so she didn't mind doing it again.

"The blankets?"

Tessa shrugged. "Maybe the restaurant is cold."

Or maybe I'm going to take you to the ocean and cuddle up with you on the bed of your truck, making sure you forget all your worries—even if just for a night, she thought, telling him to go right ahead and start the car because they didn't have all day.

Two

Jazz held the door open to the little Italian place he'd discovered, letting Tessa pass. It was different walking into a restaurant with her now than it had been back when he'd first met her.

Granted, mostly they'd been in diners, but he had a feeling it didn't change a thing.

She'd changed, had moved on from the timid girl he'd picked up at the airport that very first day.

She looked incredible, too, elegant and tempting, and Jazz couldn't help but notice men—and women—look after her as the maître d' led them to a table by the window.

They sat, and he shook his head, making her lift her brows in question. "What?" she asked, her lips distracting him for a second as he watched her lick them.

"Jazz?" she prompted, and he shook his head.

"It's crazy how you changed."

Her forehead furrowed in worry and he took her hand over the table. "Not bad, Tess. Eighteen months ago, you were walking into any public location and glancing around, nervous, your shoulders slightly slouched. You tried to not be noticed, probably wondered what people were thinking. Hell, half of the time I caught you stopping yourself in something you were doing and acting much cooler because you worried what I would think. Today you walked in here and you owned yourself. You were focused on our table, your shoulders straight. You didn't notice people staring at you, and you clearly didn't care, either. You got so much more confident, and fuck, it's sexy. If it would be a decent thing to do, I'd take you to the back right now and would fall to my knees just to please you." He'd leaned forward, had lowered his voice for the last part, and saw a blush creeping into her cheek—and lust into her eyes.

"Who cares about decent?" she replied, and he groaned, causing her to nod. "You do, true. Soldier boy and all." She grinned.

He sighed, wondering how in the world he'd gotten so lucky.

♥

The restaurant was filled to the brim, the interior decked with red in all muted and dark variations, soft violin music playing in the background, and the clutter of cutlery on plates accompanying every talk.

Tessa didn't mind. She loved the cozy corner they were seated in, and loved watching Jazz pick from the menu.

She loved watching Jazz, period.

What he'd said about her made her wonder how she hadn't noticed, and how she'd possibly appeared to him back then. Truth was, she didn't care what anyone in this restaurant thought of her because she knew Jazz loved her the way she was. Loved everything about her.

He kept reminding her of that daily, as if he'd made it his mission to prove something to her. Not that he had to. Not that he ever would have to.

It was in his gaze each and every time it settled on her.

"Did you pick?" He met her eyes and she blushed, feeling bad for having been caught.

The smile on his face told her though that he liked it. "What are you looking at, beautiful?" He wiggled his brows.

"There is this really handsome guy behind you..."

He turned, as if checking, his expression unreadable as he turned back to her and her heart sank. She wished more than anything he'd realize that he was the *only* one ever for her, and that it would stay that way.

"I was being a smartass, Jesse. You asked a dumb question and I wanted to tease you. I was looking at *you*. I've been only looking at you or for you since I met you. I don't see any others anymore."

She took his hand and pulled it up to her face, leaning into his palm. "God, it's time you and I finally say yes so all that nonsense about you fearing me walking out can stop," she added, almost furious.

Jazz stood then, only to kneel in front of her chair and place his face on his arms in her lap. She heard the silence spreading at the tables directly around them, but didn't care. What she did care about was the way he met her eyes.

"Tessa, there's never been a man who's been luckier than I am."

"Oh my, a proposal," someone whispered, and Tessa wanted to tell them they were already engaged, but kept her attention on her fiancé.

"Jesse, please," she whispered.

"How in the world did I deserve you? I should be on the ground twenty-four-seven, worshipping it because you walk on it. I can never, in my life, believe that you wouldn't be able to find someone better, and no, you saying yes won't stop me from worrying you'd walk out on me. God, taking you here was a ridiculous idea because I thought I'd be able to only hold your hand through lunch and not be near you any other way—but I can't. Let's go."

"Grab a burger at the diner and then take it to go?" she offered, and he finally smiled again, grabbing his chest.

"A woman after my own heart. Screw expensive. Let's go and have lunch in my truck."

He stood and leaned down to kiss her. She closed her eyes, hearing people chuckle and some clap, but didn't care. His kiss was unhurried, perfect, the soft strokes of his tongue igniting a fire low in her belly that she'd stoke until she could have her wicked way with him.

Afterward he held out his hand and she accepted while people still applauded them.

She shook her head once they were back outside and he drew her into his side.

"What?" he asked, and she looked up at him.

"You totally ruined Valentine's for at least half of the couples because none of the men are even half as handsome as you, and maybe a quarter as romantic. I hope you feel terrible that most of them won't get laid and will actually end up fighting."

He laughed, the tension in him finally gone, and she relaxed. She couldn't say what it was, but she was glad something had done the trick.

Once they reached his truck, she drew him in, leaning against the cold metal and wrapped her arms around his middle, meeting his ocean eyes.

"I love you."

"I love you, too," he instantly replied, cupping her cheeks. "I love you so much, I might just pass on lunch and take a bite out of you."

She giggled. "That has nothing to do with love and everything with little Jesse here." She boldly reached out and cupped him through his jeans, causing him to hiss.

"He's not little, and if you keep yourself busy with him, we'll fumble around in the backseat like love-sick teenagers," he threatened, and she blinked her lashes innocently at him.

"Promise?"

She moved her hand, rubbed his growing erection and he dropped his head forward. She liked that he gave her the chance to tease him, and since he stood close enough, no one would know what they were doing. It more looked as if they were talking.

She kissed his neck, bit the vein there, and he groaned, finally stilling her hand.

He exhaled slowly, then met her eyes. "I certainly know where your head is," he whispered, but she shook her head.

"Not yet, but you know where it will be."

Another groan escaped his lips and she smiled to herself. It wasn't the first time they'd be sleeping with each other, and it certainly hadn't been that long, but she still couldn't wait to get somewhere a little different to kiss him, tease him, and eventually be one with him.

♥

Jazz couldn't think, and the place Tessa had her hand just a few minutes earlier was majorly responsible.

It also didn't help that he felt her fingers roaming while he was driving, and so he took her hand, holding onto it before kissing the back of it. "Tessa Rowan—"

"I prefer Tessa Soon-To-Be Conner," she announced; her voice light, her smile happy.

"My dearest sweetheart—"

"Yes, forever and for always yours," she agreed, making him sigh in exasperation while she chuckled.

God, she was adorable. He hit the signal and turned into an alley, then drew Tessa closer. "Listen, you annoying woman. Don't constantly interrupt me when I'm trying to—"

And interrupted he was again, only this time she was kissing him, crawling into his lap, unbuttoning his shirt.

So much for telling her to not tease him anymore. "What in the world, sweetie?" he asked breathlessly as she kissed her way down his jaw, her hands roaming his naked chest.

"We're alone, and we have alone-time, and we don't need to rush anything because no one will interrupt us," she whispered against his skin, nearly driving him crazy.

"You do realize you're rushing? We wanted to have lunch."

She rolled her eyes. "Technicalities. I wouldn't be rushing if—"

A knock on the window interrupted them anyway, and when Jazz glanced out of the window, he had a hard time not to groan.

He rolled it down slowly.

"This is a public street and almost lunch time. What in the world do you think you're doing?" the officer asked, and Jazz tried to nudge Tessa off his lap, but she didn't budge.

"Officer," she said instead, her voice sugary sweet, her best radio voice. "It's Valentine's and his mom is watching our infant. It's been so long that we... you know... I'm so sorry, but God, I just needed to kiss him. I was so glad we'd not have rush or anything. We wanted to go for lunch, but I just..." She brought her eyes back to him, her expression full of longing. "He's so handsome, I just couldn't resist. And we'll be married soon and..."

The officer's expression had turned amused and still there was something in his eyes. He closed them. "Talk again," he ordered.

"About what? You know, love stories are kinda my—"

The officer's eyes snapped open. "You're TR! My wife and I love your show. I hadn't realized you were here, in the US, and in Monterey nonetheless!" He sounded like a little boy on Christmas and Jazz inconspicuously started to button up his shirt again while Tessa reached out of the window and shook his hand.

"Wait, then you must be Desert Heart."

Jazz's hands froze as the officer looked his way again.

I am, and also half naked and utterly embarrassed, he thought, forcing a smile.

"That I am, Sir. Corporal Jesse Connor." He nodded, finishing what he started.

"Thank you for your service. And I'm glad you and TR worked it out. My wife was glued to the radio during that time. So much pain, hopelessness…" He winked. "No wonder you couldn't wait to get anywhere decent to get your hands on your woman."

Jazz glanced briefly at said woman who was smirking smugly, looking probably innocent to people who didn't know her.

"Never can, Sir," he agreed and then drew Tessa in to press a gentle kiss to her forehead. The officer slapped his palm against the roof of the truck three times and then nodded, his smile turning serious.

"I'm passing on the parking ticket and the one for indecent exposure, but please, Corporal, take it somewhere else. Next time I won't be so lenient."

"Thank you, Officer, and tell your wife hi. What's her name? I can give her a shout-out in my next show."

The man's face lit up at that suggestion. "Danielle Dickson, she's light of my life and she will collapse hearing her name. God, thank you so much!"

Tessa nodded and then the officer left. In the rearview Jazz watched how the police cruiser vanished around the corner, and Tessa collapsed onto him, laughing until tears fell down her cheeks.

"That was horrible! I almost would've gotten in trouble because you cannot keep it together, Tessa Connor!" His heart slowed somewhat, and he watched her.

"Say that again." Her chocolate eyes were nearly black with lust.

"Tessa Connor."

She licked her lips. "Jesus, best thing ever," she mumbled and then was kissing him again, her lips demanding, wild, almost crazed on his, and he finally pulled her off his lap and placed her in her seat.

"Food, now, and then we'll see about anything else, okay?"

And he had to insist on the food because her mood had infected him, and he needed to get his hands on her skin as soon as possible.

However, they'd also need fuel just so their passion wouldn't run at out some point, and that was the first item on his list.

Three

The sun was finally setting and although Tessa had been ready to just get Jazz naked, he'd managed to make her eat and take a long walk with him along the beach, starting at their favorite vantage point.

The sand was ice cold, but Tessa had taken off her shoes anyway, loving the feel of her bare feet on the sand. Jazz had his arm around her, kissing the side of her head over and over, as if he couldn't get close enough, couldn't believe they were there.

They'd circled back to the truck and sat on the truck bed as they watched the sun vanish in the ocean.

"The first time I brought you here I wondered if I could ever find someone like you here, in my world," he whispered, and she thought back to that night sitting on his truck, comforting her best friend.

"What did you figure out?" she asked, entwining their fingers on his thigh.

"There's no one else like you. Couldn't be. I knew I wanted you from the very first kiss. Before that. Only I wasn't brave enough to go after it."

"You knew nothing about me," she pointed out, resting her head on his shoulder, her feet hanging off the ledge, kicking lazily at the cold air.

"I didn't have to. My soul recognized yours, and my heart started your beat. No touch needed. I knew everything was different from then on."

She grinned teasingly. "You turned into a poet then." Because holy shit, that man knew what to say to make her knees weak and her heart cry out with love.

"I turned into *your* man then."

She shifted, nudging him backward until he sat in the middle of the truck, and she climbed back onto his lap, holding his gaze.

He lifted his hand and pulled her hair free, the blonde waves cascading around her shoulders, then he cupped her cheek and drew her in. Softly he kissed the corner of her mouth, then the other side, his gestures so infinitely tender, Tessa wanted to weep.

"I." *Kiss.* "Love." *Very long kiss.* "You." He shook his head, his face close enough so his nose touched hers. "So much, Tessa. So incredibly much."

"Make love to me. Here. Now. All night. We have enough blankets to keep us covered, and if I leave my bra on, we might not get into trouble."

They had tested their luck once already, but Jazz had been right that morning. This was the perfect place, with the ocean playing its soft symphony, and the stars sparkling above them like freshly cut diamonds.

"Tessa," he whispered, but she didn't care, didn't let him finish his protest. Instead she claimed his mouth and, opening his jacket before letting his shirt follow, made sure he knew what she was out for. He shivered, but she didn't let him suffer long. Moving on, she wrapped her arms around him and pressing her lips onto his again, teasing his tongue, licking into his mouth until he groaned, wrapping her hair into a ponytail and pulling her head back softly. He nipped at her exposed neck, then his hands took off her jacket, too, and the sweater with the same movement, and wrapped a blanket around them both.

"You really want it here," he muttered, and she nodded, slowing their heated make-out-session to brush her fingertips across his skin.

"I want you, and I want you to remember that after all this time, after everything, it's you and me, Jazz. We're not exactly the same people we were back when being here the very first time, but we're together. Just like that day. And in fifty years, we'll still be together. Here, at this place. It'll always be just us, Jazz. Us together."

She couldn't remember one occasion when it hadn't been them here. Even when she'd run, run from everything because she'd been overwhelmed during his recovery, he'd found her there, had been with her there.

This place held only good memories for her, and she knew that if she ever needed a reminder of how it felt to be utterly in love with him, and why, she'd only have to come here—with him, and they'd know. It would be their spot forever and a day.

♥

Jazz lowered his eyes, wondering why Tessa always knew how to make him feel good. Switching positions with her, he tasted her skin, took his time until she was quivering, and not because of the cold.

"I feel like this is our first ever real date, and I'm messing up by trying to convince you to fumble around in my truck because my mom is not supposed to catch us," he suddenly muttered, resting his forehead against her stomach, and she laughed, wrapping her hands around his head and drawing him up.

"Remember? I started this game. And I'll keep going." He felt how her hands left his face and then went between their bodies, where she opened his jeans and then reached into his boxers, wrapping her fingers around his erection.

Why in the world did he allow her to take the lead when he'd been longing to seduce her, to make her see stars when being with him? Instead it was him thinking he'd die before he ever reached his orgasm. Her hands were sure, proving she knew him better than anyone else, and she had him where she wanted it within minutes. The expression on her face made that more than clear.

"Kick off those pants, soldier, and while you're at it, how about you help me out of mine, too?"

Oh, and he would. She was way too relaxed and collected. He vanished under the blankets, making sure she was covered up to her shoulders. He worried because, holy shit, they could get in a hell of a lot trouble for this, but if Tessa wanted it, he sure wouldn't tell her no.

God, was there anything he'd turn down if she wanted it? Probably not.

Her pants were off while he kicked his own deeper. He didn't want to take his hands from her. Instead he found her sweet spot—and her ready for him—but he wanted to tease her a little bit.

"Jesse," she whispered as he licked along her thigh and then her hip bones, across to the other leg before parting them and running the tip of his tongue along her middle. She gasped, her hands finding their way into his hair. "God, please."

He had no idea what she was asking for, but it didn't matter, either. Holding her with his hands, he teased and tasted her until he knew she was close. Pushing two fingers into her, he continued teasing her, bringing her to the brink he wanted her on, and it was only when her grip on him got stronger that he gave in and moved up until he could kiss her lips. He didn't stop his fingers, and used his thumb to do what his tongue no longer could, but she shook her head.

"Please, Jesse, I need you inside of me. I need you now. Hold me close. Become one with me. *Be* one with me," she pleaded.

"God, Tess." He wanted it, desperately, but he already knew it wouldn't hold long once she was wrapped all around him. She'd been teasing him too much that day, had gotten him too close around noon, and he'd been ready to have her then.

"Yes," she urged as she felt him shift, and he bit his lips, lowering himself between her legs, moving forward in a long, lazy stroke that drove him nearly insane.

Being with Tessa never got old. This wasn't their first ride. Hell, it wasn't even their tenth ride, and yet he didn't tire of feeling her under him, of looking at her and drowning in her mere presence.

Their dance was erotic, slow and sensual, and as she wrapped her legs around him, urging him deeper, faster, he gave in.

He kissed her then, his eyes closed, and rocked her to the sound of the waves hitting the shore.

It was almost as if the entire universe came together to make this night more special than any had ever been before.

♥

Tessa listened to Jazz's heartbeat, expecting it to slowly calm down, but it didn't happen. Resting her chin on her hand on his chest, she met his eyes in the pale moonlight. He looked content, happy, and it was something she didn't see too often.

"It was as if the universe approved. No interruptions, no noise besides the ocean and you, and a million sparkling stars. This was meant to be, and by this, I mean us, in this place, at this time," he whispered.

He'd changed since the first time they'd been there, had gotten more serious, more reflective and yet she loved him more than ever. She probably had changed, too, but didn't know, couldn't say for sure because well, people hardly ever dissected themselves as much as they did the people they loved.

"That's because we *do* belong together. I was meant to be late, and then early that day at the airport, and you were meant to find me. A hundred-people passed me, and no one cared. You literally fell for me. It was the universe speaking even back then already."

He smiled, cupping her cheek and shifting until he could kiss her sweetly.

"I'm glad we didn't disappoint the universe."

She grinned. "Yeah, so am I."

(Never) The End

Wanna know more about Jazz and Tessa?
Start their journey in Tagged For Life, Tagged Soldiers #1

This Soldier's Heart
Bella Sterling

I carry your kiss within my heart
Doesn't matter how long we're apart

It won't be long, love, and we'll be together again

I keep going, push through the fear
Just endure

Despite the pain of not having you here
You are what keeps me pushing through the fear

Your face is a photograph that won't fade, kept in my heart
To be taken out and pored over on the long nights

I haven't held your hand in one hundred and eighty-four days
Your letters carry the scent of your skin
And bring the beauty of your smile into sharp relief

This Soldier's Heart

Miles may keep us apart
But I carry your kiss within my heart
Along with your smile, the way it lights up a room
It brightens my mind whenever I think of you
I cannot feel your heat anywhere near
But the touch of your skin is a memory I hold dear
Your scent is seared into my brain
The imprint of your lips what keeps me sane
You're always on my mind and in my dreams
Your face the only thing that feels real

A Soldier's Enchantment
C.M. Lehsten

1

May 5, 1945
Innsbruck, Austria

As the sun burned the morning fog from the valley below, John Lemp began to see the Inn River materialize in the first morning light. The river looked serene from this height and he could just about pretend it was any number of the smaller rivers at home instead of the Austrian countryside.

The war was nearly over. After months of riding in the tank for endless hours, marching mile after mile, fighting battle upon battle, the end was in sight. It felt like a decade had passed since he'd worked the family farm with his father in the fields. High school felt like another lifetime instead of the few short years it had been. John prayed for the day he would make it home to his parents' house in the Hudson River Valley of northern New York. Although this was the land of his great grandparents, it wasn't the home he longed for. The smell of the lilacs that would be blooming in his mother's garden just about now, the smell of the freshly plowed earth. He missed his mother's fresh baked cookies, his father's French toast and maple syrup for breakfast, along with real coffee. What he wouldn't give for a cup of coffee that didn't taste like dirt.

His Lieutenant was confident they would be home before the end of the month. God, he hoped it was true. His bones ached from the endless bouncing and jarring. His heart had been shattered a million times over by the atrocities he had witnessed. There were rumors that the Fuhrer was dead, but the Allied forces were yet to confirm the hearsay.

The rest of the battalion began to stir as the sun's first rays were beginning to bring the other side of the valley into clear detail. The dew on the grass was evaporating slowly. He knew the temperature wouldn't rise enough to get rid of the chill in the air today. He pulled his collar up over his ears, his buzzed blonde hair doing nothing to warm his body. Another long and cold day was ahead of them.

Yesterday they were to be relieved by the 36th infantry division, but late in the night a man had run into camp pleading with his Lieutenant to intercede and save a group that were being held hostage by the Reich in a castle not far from their position. It looked like another battle was in their path. The lieutenant was waiting for word from HQ whether they would still be relieved or if they would be going on to Castle Itter. John had overheard parts of the conversation. It sounded like there were a bunch of dignitaries and important people being held at this castle but not many soldiers guarding them. It shouldn't be too difficult of a fight if they were sent but every battle held the potential to be the last.

"Yo! Ice get down here," came the yell from the gunman. John had gotten the nickname "Ice" from the glacial blue of his eyes within days of joining the army. He answered to it almost as quickly as he did to John and since the Lieutenant was *also* a John, nicknames made it easier.

"On my way." John poured out the dirt tasting coffee and walked slowly to the tank. Word must have come from HQ as he saw the rest of the battalion gather around the Lieutenant.

♥

2

Castle Itter, Austria

The castle garden was just coming to life. Ida could see the well-formed leaves and tiny buds forming on the trees and flowers. Spring was her favorite part of the year with all the new life blooming and bursting from mother earth. She could smell the fresh scent of dirt, grass, even the animals on the crisp morning breeze. The crocuses had already begun to poke their purple heads through the light morning frost, their leaves glistening in the early sun. As she checked on the many animal and plant inhabitants in the garden Ida considered the people currently being held in the castle by the Reich. Some were famous, some just thought themselves important. Most of the servants were Austrian countrymen who had been forced into servitude by the SS soldiers. Ida knew none of them would matter if she failed in her mission.

Her mother and sisters had sent her from their home in the Harz mountains several days travel from Castle Itter to keep the book of spells out of the hands of the Reich. She chose Castle Itter as the hiding place because there were not many soldiers compared to prisoners and servants. Plus, no one would think something valuable would be hidden in an occupied castle that was serving as a prison. She had been here for the last year but the time to leave was drawing near. Her family did not know her exact hiding place, believing it best that only she knew where the book was hidden.

This was not the first time in her young life she had been sent away from her home to fulfill a mission. She had been on gathering trips all over Europe to harvest herbs as well as spending time with a band of gypsies to determine how much magic they truly practiced. With her long dark tresses and emerald colored eyes, she blended in well among the nomadic people. It turned out they knew a few spells even her people did not. Ida had surpassed her older sister's abilities by the time she had returned home a year later.

As she sat on the stone bench with her heavy basket of laundry a small rabbit poked his head out of his burrow. Ida wiggled her pinky finger as she whispered, "*Guten morgen kleiner bruder*, I see you there." The rabbit slowly moved toward her, looking around wearily as he went. As he approached, Ida bent forward and laid her hand on the ground. He crawled into her palm. She lifted him slowly with a smile curving her lips.

"Aren't you a handsome fellow, little brother?" She blew him a gentle kiss. "Back to your momma and siblings with you, so I can get my chores done," she said as she lowered him back to the ground. "Thank you for visiting me this morning, precious."

Ida climbed to her feet and walked over to the wash basin. She scrubbed the linens and sang softly as the sun came up over the hills surrounding the castle. Within a few minutes, several birds and the rest of the rabbits were mesmerized by her movements and the sound of her voice. Lost in her song and her chore, she didn't notice until she bent to empty the wash water.

"Well, look at all the company mother earth has brought me this morning!" she exclaimed when she finally turned around. "I don't suppose any of you would like to hang these linens for me? No, I didn't think so," she laughed as she hung the linens to dry. The sun was nearly fully overhead when she wished the animals a good day and returned to the interior of the castle.

Today was the day the runes had foretold. There would be bloodshed, victories, and losses today. Just a few days ago, on Walpurgisnacht, what many called "witches night," Ida had learned that this mission was not just about protecting the book. On the night when the veil between the living and the dead was quite thin, her great-great-great grandmother had shown Ida that she would meet her soulmate today. The father of her children, the future of her people. She had seen his face in her dreams as long as she could remember, and it was comforting to her to finally know why he had always lived in her dreams but not her everyday life. She knew every lash of his eyes and every hair on his head from the many years of dreams. She didn't know how she would meet him, but she could already feel his energy nearby and was stronger for it than she had ever been. She was full of energy, hope and her youth as she began her indoor chores.

♥

3

Innsbruck, Austria
John

As I had believed would happen, HQ ordered us to liberate the VIPs that were being held at Castle Itter some 45 miles away. Our relief was set to join us in the siege.

Camp was broken quickly, and my battalion started our slow trek to the small castle.

As we entered a small village, gunfire broke out. The company took cover holding fire. We had seen this scenario many times over the previous months. Villagers took up arms to defend themselves against an attack by the Reich and trusted no troops that entered their borders. We had long since established the strategy of waiting out their ammunition instead of returning fire on innocent civilians. When the gunfire ceased, a lone man approached. He told the Lieutenant that the Commandant of Castle Itter had left early that morning for Dachau. The man was leading a small group of Austrian resistance fighters that wanted to join in freeing the castle. About thirty men joined us as our march to the castle continued.

♥

4

Castle Itter
Ida

When I returned to the castle, chaos reigned. The commandant had been seen leaving the castle with the few SS troops that had been stationed within the castle while I had been washing the linens. The French VIP prisoners were arming themselves with anything they could find—guns, bows, axes, even a few ancient torches and decorative battle axes determined to free themselves from captivity. The Austrian servants were already running out the doors and lining the windows in case more troops were being sent. Everywhere I looked were people with weapons. It seemed confusion and terror reigned within the stone walls. I was breathing hard with my heart in my throat as I approached Hans, one of the Austrians who had always been nice to me. Grabbing his arm as he passed, I cried, "Hans, what is going on? I just stepped into the gardens to hang the wash and madness broke out inside the walls."

"Commandant Schwimmer has fled. We are preparing to take back the castle ourselves while we have the chance. The emissary we sent to the village never returned but the Commandant at Dachau has died. Schwimmer said he received word just before first light that he is to take the position immediately. But I do not believe that is the case. I believe that he is scared because he knows the Reich is falling to the Allied forces and he ran for his life. However, the SS Troops at Dachau may decide we need detaining again once they realize Schwimmer has left us mostly unguarded."

I turned from Hans and dashed up the castle stairs as quickly as I could. I knew that he was right, the SS Troops would be coming to retake the castle and its important prisoners. I didn't know if my love was to be an SS soldier or an Allied soldier or even an Austrian countryman. All I knew was that I could feel him getting closer. It was like a comforting heat in each of my veins. I felt invigorated and bursting with energy. I needed to get to the top levels to determine which way my soulmate was approaching from.

♥

5

John

I could see the castle coming into view as we crested the hill. Its beautiful white walls were stunning in the bright sunlight, nothing like a prison at all. I had learned over the months of warfare not to be surprised by what the Reich was capable of turning ugly, but it was still shocking to me that the quaint and beautiful castle could be turned into a prison. I felt the calmness of battle come over me. Some soldiers became anxious before a battle, I became calm. Everything became crystal clear and slow motion for me as we prepared for battle.

I began identifying entry points and likely hiding places for the enemy. We were still a few miles from the Castle when I began to feel strange. It had been months since my feet felt warm unless we were sitting around a fire but suddenly my toes were a comfortable temperature. My cheeks felt flushed as if I had just been embarrassed. As I took inventory of my body, I realized that I was not even chilled. It felt as though I had a heat source in the middle of my chest set to just the right temperature. There was no fear associated with the feeling, instead there was only comfort. I was still trying to figure out what was causing these odd sensations within my body when we began descending into the last valley separating us from the castle.

Seemingly out of nowhere we began taking fire from machine guns and tanks on the opposite side of the valley. We scrambled to get into defensive position, but I counted at least 5 of our men struck down in those initial rounds. I stopped along the side of the road next to Jimmy Moffett. He and I had quickly become friends when we learned our hometowns were less than 50 miles from each other. He had been shot in the leg just above the knee. Moving quickly, I ripped off my belt and tied it around Jimmy's leg to slow the bleeding.

"Go, stay with the battalion!" Jimmy said as I tightened the belt.

"No, I won't leave you here alone."

"Go! The lieutenant and the other men are counting on you Ice. I'll be fine, I promise." Jimmy held up his own gun to demonstrate that he was not defenseless. "You'll catch me after you win the battle."

Just then Nate Stevens came running back to us and helped me get Jimmy up on the back of one of the slow-moving tanks. It would be a painful ride, but he would be protected until we could get him better medical treatment. We marched on behind the tank swinging our heads constantly to watch for more enemy fire.

♥

6

Ida

I heard the gunfire followed by sporadic artillery explosions as I raced up the steps. My heart began thudding in my chest. What if I were to meet my love only to have him die on the first day? Nothing in the runes or my great-great-great grandmother's words guaranteed a long future between us, only that we would meet today. As the daughter of the high priestess and the most powerful among my people it had been assumed that I would live a long life with children to carry on our traditions, but my fear was overriding my certainty.

I reached the top of the tower and looked out over the valleys that circled the castle. About 10 kilometers to the east, I spotted a large group of soldiers hiding behind tanks and trucks. I could also see SS Troops hiding in the thin cover of bushes and trees on the castle side of the valley preparing to fire again on the advancing Allied troops. They had arrived to take back the castle just as the Allied troops were coming to our rescue.

I raced back down the stairs shouting to the inhabitants of the castle. "Our rescuers are coming but the SS are attacking them! To arms people! Help the Allied forces to free us all!" My voice rang out through the entire castle from the basements to the highest battlements.

When I reached the ground floor, several of the German servants ran to the outer wall of the castle and lifted the gate. They poured out into the surrounding forest and gunfire soon rang out from their weapons.

I ran after them, disregarding the danger of the gunfight. I rushed down the hill hiding behind the sparse trees and following the pull that was like a magnet in my heart. As I reached the bottom of the valley and began the climb up the opposite hill. I was being guided by instincts alone. I could hear the yells of orders and agony from both sides.

I was closing in on the Allied troops when I spotted *him,* and everything in my world slowed down.

♥

7

John

I was surrounded by the sounds of gunfire and artillery explosions as we advanced down the hill. I could see the castle looming on the next hilltop. The feeling of warmth and comfort was growing stronger with each foot of progress we made toward the castle. It had suddenly begun to increase in the last few minutes. As puzzled as I was by the feeling, my focus was on protecting my fellow soldiers and myself. The SS troops were very close now, so close we could hear their yells between gunfire. We were nearly to the bottom of the valley when I felt a sting in my left thigh. My steps faltered, and I fell to my knees. I looked down to see blood pouring out of the bullet hole midway between my hip and knee. Time seemed to stand still, and the sounds of the battle faded as I looked at my wound. As I watched the blood flow from my wound, the pain I expected to feel did not come but the feeling of comfort grew. Maybe I was destined to die in this battle and the feeling of comfort was what death felt like.

I'm not ready to die! I had my whole life in front me and I wasn't going to let this war rob me of it. I tore my uniform shirt and began wrapping the wound to slow the blood flow. Before I got the fabric around my leg, I saw the wound getting smaller and the sounds of battle seemed farther away. It closed completely, leaving only the bloody mess on my pants and a small star shaped scar. I looked up and saw the most beautiful woman running toward me. There was a soft glow around her, and bullets bounced off it like a shield.

I looked around, trying to figure out if I was shell shocked or if I had gone deaf. Or crazy. That was definitely possible. The battle was in full swing on every side of me, yet no one else noticed this entrancing woman in our midst. She neared and everything around us slowed down. The men of my battalion became like statues while bullets slowed and then stopped in midair. The area became silent.

The woman ran to where I was kneeling and laid her hand on the wound that was now healed. She smiled as I felt heat on my leg where the bullet had entered. Pulling her hand away she showed me the bullet in the palm of her hand.

"I didn't want this to stay in your leg," she said as she threw the bullet to the side. "My name is Ida. I was afraid I wouldn't get here in time," she told me in the most melodious voice. The sound of her speaking to me brought a profound peace and sense of wellbeing to me at once. It was like sitting in a sun filled meadow at the height of spring.

"I know this is going to sound strange to you, but we are soul mates. I've seen you in my dreams since I was a young girl and I have felt your essence close to me for several hours. I heard the battle and knew I had to come at once."

"Am I dead? Why is everything frozen and silent? How can we be soul mates? Are you some kind of angel, or demon?" I fired the questions at her.

She laughed, "No, you are not dead. You are not even wounded. I healed you and stopped time around us. I am a witch born of the Harz mountains. This is also why I know that we are soul mates. Can't you feel it? It's like a warming sensation and comfort when we are near each other. It's like when you put the last piece of a puzzle into the whole. Now that we have met it will be painful to be without each other for long periods of time. It has been this way for my people for all of our history."

"I don't understand. Witches don't exist. *Magic* doesn't exist," I insisted.

"Oh, I assure you magic and witches most certainly exist." She raised her hand and whispered some words I could not catch. A dove appeared in the palm of her hand. One minute her hand was empty, and the next the bird was cooing gently within inches of my face. "I am the daughter of our High Priestess. Not all of my people are quite as powerful as my mother and I, nor does everyone know as many spells as we do. However, all of my people have magic within them."

She stood and raised her hand. The dove flew to a nearby tree branch and watched us. She held out her hand to me and I could not resist grasping it. When our skin touched I felt a tingling sensation. It wasn't painful or unpleasant, in fact it was exhilarating. The way her eyes widened at our contact, I knew it was a new sensation for her as well.

"What the hell was that?" I asked without releasing her hand.

"I'm not sure. I believe it is because our souls are connected. I've never felt that with anyone." She looked distracted as she added, "We need to get out of here. It is dangerous to keep this battle frozen for much longer."

"I can't leave. My place is here with my fellow soldiers." The idea of my leaving the battle was preposterous. These men had saved my life many times and their lives were in grave danger. I couldn't just walk away.

"My love, the outcome of the battle has already been determined. Whether you are here or not, the Reich will not win this battle, nor the war. But if I release my spell and am found here I may be taken prisoner by either side. I cannot risk this. If I continue to hold the spell, there will be damage done to the minds of all the men held within it. I do not wish to harm any of them. I cannot risk your life either. You are my future," she pleaded with me as she began backing toward the castle, pulling me with her.

Looking into her eyes, I could not deny the connection we had. I could feel her pulse through our joined hands. I felt more alive and rejuvenated than I had ever experienced.

"Can you keep them safe? Make sure none of my battalion dies in this battle?" I asked her, still resisting the idea of leaving.

"I cannot. I can heal the wounded after the battle but those who are meant to leave this world will do so. I'm afraid I cannot interfere with that. It delves into dark magic and is against our laws."

I let go of her hand, looking at the many who were already wounded. I felt the change the instant my skin was no longer in contact with hers and already felt the absence of our physical connection, but I needed to help my friends.

"Can you heal the ones who are wounded now, like Jimmy?" I begged. I feared he had lost too much blood. I was still trying to wrap my mind around the existence of witches, but my own healed wound was evidence of her power. I knew I couldn't help but go with her wherever she led but I needed to do what I could to help my battalion.

"Yes, my love, that I can do," she smiled as she walked over to where Jimmy lay frozen on the backside of the tank.

The woman, Ida, approached the back of the tank where Jimmy lay. As she had with me, she laid her hand on his injured leg and closed her eyes, chanting too softly for me to understand her words. A soft blue glow surrounded her hand, becoming gradually brighter. Her voice was comforting and melodic. After a short time, she drew her hand away. I saw that his wound was completely healed. The only evidence of injury was the blood on his pants.

I watched while she walked around the battlefield and healed several others in the same way. After she had seen to all the superficial wounds she came back to where I was still standing.

"Come, we must leave this place. I need to return to the castle and retrieve my family book and then we will go into the mountains," she said as she held out her hand to me.

Although I desperately wanted to feel her touch again, I was hesitant to leave my fellow soldiers. I looked around at the faces of the men that had become my family. This was crazy. I didn't know this woman. I was a soldier, sworn to stand in battle. I could not desert my battalion.

"I know you don't wish to leave them, but they will be victorious. And no one will realize you have not been here. After this victory the war will end shortly. Our destiny is not here in this valley, nor at Castle Itter. Our destiny is with each other."

"I can't just leave them here. My duty is to my country and these men. I don't know you. I know *them*. I know the causes we are fighting for. I've seen the atrocities the Reich is committing. I cannot abandon my duty," I protested.

"I respect your commitment and your honor. Your presence or absence here will not change the outcome. The Allied Forces have already won the war. The Fuhrer is dead. Come, my love, we must go home."

"My home is on another continent. Look, you seem to mean well, and I admit that there is something between us but I'm not leaving my battalion like this," I reiterated.

"I'm sorry, I said that wrong. We must return to my home after I retrieve the spell book from Castle Itter. I must return it to my mother for safekeeping. Then you and I can spend some time together to get to know each other. I know that we are soul mates, but I understand that this is new to you. I have dreamed of you since I was a child. Because of my heritage I have the advantage of feeling that I know you. I want to know the real you and explore this connection between us. I want to build love and trust between us. I don't know if we will stay in the mountains with my family or return to your family, but I do know our destinies are entwined."

I could not deny the connection between us. A part of me felt that I did know her, that I knew her long before I laid eyes on her just moments ago. It was crazy, but with her assurances that my battalion would win the battle, I wanted to go with her.

I took her hand and we walked to the castle.

♥

8

Ida

He was so generous and caring. My mate had asked me to save the men he was fighting beside before we departed. I knew I could not interfere with those destined to die today, but I could lessen the suffering of those only wounded.

As we approached the castle, I silently extended the time stopping spell upon the castle inhabitants. I wanted to retrieve the book and leave unobserved. I went straight to the tower from which I originally observed the battle begin. Three stairs from the top I stopped and removed a loose stone to retrieve the book.

"I am going to use a spell to take us to my family. It is several days travel if I do not use magic. Will you allow me to transport us there?" I asked him.

He looked torn for a moment before reaching his decision. "Sure, why not. I've already seen you heal several people. Obviously magic does exist and you can do amazing things."

I closed my eyes and recited the spell while holding his hand and clutching the book with the other. I felt the air shimmer around us and the smell changed to that of my mountain home. Fresh spruce and earth invaded my senses.

I opened my eyes and started walking toward my mother's cabin.

♥

9

John

Wow! That was all I could think. One minute Ida was holding my hand in a stairwell within the castle I had been charged to liberate just this morning. She started speaking some German words that I didn't understand and the next thing I knew, my surroundings started to spin and blur. In a moment, we were no longer in the castle but in a mountain forest.

I was stunned and disoriented. She started walking toward a cabin some fifty yards in front of us and I stumbled over some tree roots before I realized I had moved. Quickly righting myself, I walked by her side. Clearly, she knew where she was going and what she was doing. Her hand was still in mine, the tingling felt perfectly normal now. It heightened my senses. I could smell the spruce trees, the grass, the little white flowers that were peeking through the needle-strewn forest floor. Her skin was soft and warm, and the size of her hand was perfectly fit to the inside of mine. The feeling was difficult to explain even to myself. It felt like home. It felt like everything in the world was right and good.

She turned to look at me and smiled. I felt my heart skip a beat and then speed up at the sight of the twinkle in her eye. She was truly the most beautiful creature I had ever laid eyes on. My breath caught in my throat and the world melted away when our eyes met. Time stopped completely and only the two of us existed. I could feel our future together. I didn't know I had moved until my hand was on her cheek. Slowly I bent my head toward hers knowing only that I needed to kiss her.

Our lips met, and my heart exploded into millions of pieces all within my chest. I had goosebumps and flutters danced in my stomach. I needed to be closer to her, to feel her body pressed against mine. Our hands were both joined at our sides as I stepped into the kiss, feeling the soft outline of her body against mine. I could hear and feel her heartbeat sync with my own.

The sound of someone clearing their throat broke through the spell our kiss created. With my head still spinning and my knees wobbly, I looked toward the cabin to see an older version of Ida. If her hair was not white, I would have sworn they were twins.

♥

10

Ida

I broke away from our first kiss like a guilty child when my mother cleared her throat. My cheeks were flushed, and my head was spinning. Kissing John was like nothing I had ever experienced. My mother had tried to explain to me that every interaction with my mate would be different than with any other person, but she failed to convey how powerful and magical the connection between us would be. Even as I tried to focus on my mother, I was hungry for the next touch of our lips.

My mother stood at the door to her cabin watching us as I dragged my gaze from John.

"Ida, my darling, where is the book?" she asked quietly with raised eyebrows.

"It's lovely to see you as well, Mother," I replied sweetly as I reached into my shawl to retrieve the book. I walked over to her, noticing that John kept pace with me as I approached her.

"I trust everything went according to plan," her voice never shifted as she reached out to hug me. John started to step between us, probably concerned by the ice in her tone. I smiled at him, giving his arm the smallest of caresses to let him know it was okay as I moved into my mother's embrace. It was easy to misinterpret my mother's voice as disapproving and cold because of a spell that had gone wrong in her youth. As a result, her voice had ceased to convey her feelings. Since she had been a teenager, one had to rely on her facial features and knowing her closely to interpret her moods correctly.

"Yes, Mother. I had no problems at Castle Itter until the battle broke out today." I proceeded to tell her about the battle and finding John.

"You risked much to bring this man here, my daughter. I understand the pull to your soul mate, but to bring him to my home could endanger all of us. I will ready your cabin with the *idő kerzeitramn* spell. This way our family remains safe while you and your mate *bereite dich auf die ehe vor.*" She turned toward John. "I'm sorry, young man. I do not know your name and I am not trying to be rude. I do not know your language well. I am afraid Ida will have to translate words that I do not yet know," she admitted, blushing lightly.

"I don't think the spell does translate directly, but it means that she is going make my cabin invisible and slow time within my cabin. For every day that we spend in my cabin, one minute will have passed outside of it. You and I will only age for the time that passes outside my cabin. If we spend a week in my cabin we will age 7 minutes." I turned toward my mother and kissed her cheek. "Thank you, *Mutter*." She nodded and disappeared without so much as a leaf moving.

    I led John through the woods, choosing to take the long route to my cabin instead of the magical shortcut my mother had taken. We passed my mother's cabin and skirted around the edge of our small village. I felt introducing John to all of our village would be too overwhelming after pulling him from the battle and exposing my magic. The trees grew thicker and the shadows of the forest turned slightly darker as we walked farther from the village.

    After a few moments, the shadows thinned again, and we could hear the trickle to the stream that ran alongside my cabin. We emerged into my clearing and I was thrilled to see mother had cared for my tiny garden while I had been at Castle Itter. The wild mixture of color from my crocus made me smile. The bright orange, purple, yellow, pink and pristine white filled me with the energy of spring and the happiness of warm sunlight.

    I stole a sideways glance at John, wanting to see his reaction to my tiny hideaway that had become my own slice of heaven. I had worked hard during the 3 years since moving out of my mother's cabin into my own to make this place a home that would nurture my spirit.

    John's smile reached his whole face. I noticed a dimple in his chin for the first time and his eyes sparkled. My heart raced, a feeling of completeness coming over me that this man would find joy in my simple home.

    My mother stood to the side of my door with her hands raised and chanting softly. Her skirt swirled slowly at her bare feet as they floated just above the ground. Leaves began to stir through my small garden circling my cabin. The air shimmered turning slightly blue, then pink in a bubble surrounding the entire building as rays of light the same colors seemed to spray harmlessly into the woods as far as I could see. My mother's voice became louder as her body floated higher above the earth. When she was floating even with my front windows, the shimmer of the air turned green and then violet. She continued to rise as her voice grew in volume. As she reached the height of my roof the shimmer in the air swirled with all of the previous colors creating a vortex around the cabin. The rays of color seemed to touch the sky and reach endlessly into the woods around us.

Slowly, my mother descended back to the earth. The swirling colors dimmed and shrank into my cabin as her feet touched the ground, a slight opaque waviness remained around in the air.

"You may both enter now. The spell encompasses a circular area from the *Braunwasserbach* to the village with its center here. You may travel anywhere within during your time here. Once either of you leave the sphere of the spell, time will be restored to its natural course," my mother said, focusing mostly on John. She turned quickly and strode into the woods towards her own cabin.

I moved forward with John who was wide-eyed and quiet. I wondered what was going through his mind. I felt bad for how quickly he had been thrown from his world of science and logic into my world of spells, magic and ancient customs. I was looking forward to learning more about his family, his likes and dislikes, his dreams and to sharing mine with him.

♥

11

John

My eyes were stunned. I was having a hard time believing that this was reality. Maybe I had been shot during the battle and this was some pain induced hallucination. Not since I was four or five years-old had I believed that anything like this could exist in the world. Ida, as beautiful as she was, was also apparently a powerful witch who could pull magic out of the thin German air. Her mother seemed to be much more powerful than even Ida. She had just been floating some fifteen feet off the ground while the air swirled with the colors of the rainbow all around us. I watched her walk into the woods in the direction we had come from as I tried to process all that had happened today. I was a soldier far from my home fighting a monstrous enemy responsible for millions of horrific deaths. For months my life consisted of marching, gunfire, gore and tragedy nearly every minute of the day. I wished fervently that the war had been just a nightmare. My experiences here would haunt me until my dying day.

But the war was real. *This* was real. Somehow, magic existed.

I shook my head and brought my focus back to my surroundings. The small cabin in front of us was the picture of charming. Hundreds of crocuses decorated the front wall in every hue imaginable. The small flowers and the quaint cabin made a joyful picture to my mind. I could imagine living here happily if not for my family being on the other side of the world.

The thought of my family made me homesick. Ida had told me earlier that the war was nearly over. I hoped that was true, so I could see my mother and father soon.

I shook off the melancholy of missing my family and turned to Ida. Although I had met her only a few short hours ago I could not deny the connection I felt with her. When our eyes met, my heart beat faster, my palms were sweaty, and I had butterflies in my stomach. Any time we touched there was a warmth and the tingling sensation. Just being close to her I could physically feel where she was without actually seeing her. I realized I was looking forward to exploring these sensations and spending time with her.

"Come," Ida said as she started toward the cabin. "You must be hungry."

We walked through the door into a large main room. The hearth was in front of us in the center or the room. A large fire was already ablaze in the hearth. To the left was a heavy wooden table surrounded by four chairs. There were shelves lining the outside of the room lined with various sized bowls and pots. To the right was a sitting area with a large comfortable sofa and chair facing the hearth. A knitting basket sat next to the chair and several warm quilts were scattered on the furniture. The floor was bare wood that had been worn to a smooth finish. There was a door on the right behind the sofa that I assumed led to a bedroom.

Ida gestured to the table as she moved over to the hearth removing a large pot that had been hanging above the fire. She spooned stew into two wooden bowls and sat down next to me at the table.

My stomach growled loudly as the delicious smell of the stew reached my nose. Ida chuckled quietly and dug into her own bowl. Blushing slightly, I began to eat. We ate in companionable silence for several minutes.

After eating, we moved over to the comfortable furniture and sat next to each other on the sofa. We started to tell each other stories of our childhood. If you discarded the different location and the magic in Ida's bloodline, our upbringing was not all that different.

Although my parent's roles were reversed from her parents, the morals and strictness of discipline was the same in both households. In my family, my father took the dominant role and worked many hours to pay our bills. My parents worshiped each other, they were equal partners with their own strengths and weaknesses. Throughout my childhood they had taught me that love and respect was the solid foundation on which to build a marriage. In Ida's family, her mother was dominant while her father took care of the younger children and the household chores. Her mother was the leader and devoted many hours each day to the running of the village. She heard disputes, tended the ill, assisted new mothers in childbirth, oversaw the crops and water gathering. I was fascinated by the differences in our cultures as well as the similarities. We talked well into the night and both fell asleep on the couch.

  I woke up with bright sunshine filtering into the cabin through the windows. As I sat up to stretch, Ida brought me a steaming mug of fresh coffee. Smiling sweetly, she returned to the kitchen area without a word. After a few sips of coffee, I walked out the front door to further stretch my cramped muscles. My body was used to marching every day, not sitting and talking for hours on end. I wandered around each side of the cabin noting the outhouse in the back for later use. I stopped by the stream that was running along the right side and splashed my face with the cool water. Alongside the back of the cabin, I found the outhouse and several storage buildings, a smoke house and a stock of firewood. I made a mental note to bring in firewood later.

  I turned left again to walk along the last side of the cabin and Ida was there. She was sitting cross legged on the ground and held her finger to her lips as I approached her. She pointed out into the forest and I saw a mother lynx with three small cubs. I gently lowered myself to the ground next to Ida and watched as the cubs tumbled and played while their mother bathed whichever cub ended up with in tongue's reach.

  "Is this safe?" I asked as quietly as I could into Ida's ear.

  "Absolutely. The wildlife will not harm me, nor those with me no matter how fierce the animal. My kind are always friends with all living creatures." Her response was just as low as my question. She reached out and took my hand in hers as we continued to watch the cats in the morning sun.

After a while, the cats got bored with their spot or they got hungry. Something made them wander away from Ida's cabin and we returned inside where Ida had prepared breakfast. We chatted about different animals as we ate, and I cleaned up with directions from Ida.

Once the dishes and food were cleared we walked down to the river that ran nearby. We took our time as Ida pointed out the different plants that she and her people used in potions and spells. At the river, we fished for a few hours until we had plenty for our lunch and walked back to the cabin.

There was no awkward silence between us. One topic of conversation flowed easily into another. Before I knew it, we had supper and cleaned up together. That evening, we fell asleep on the couch the same as the evening before.

Several days passed in the same fashion as that first. We spent every minute together. As the days passed, we held hands more often and the tingling seemed to settle into a warmth and overall feeling of safety and comfort. On the fourth day, we had been picking wild flowers for an hour or so when Ida began laughing at something I had said. Her laugh was contagious and before we knew it both of us were laying on the ground holding our stomachs from laughing so hard. We rolled toward each other and the laughter slowly receded as our eyes met.

I tilted my head toward her, our mouths finally touching in our first kiss. In that kiss, I felt our souls join. All else ceased to matter. This beautiful woman who wielded magic as easily as some people changed clothes was everything to me. I knew that I would do anything to make her happy and protect her for the rest of my life.

Whether she came to my country or I moved to Germany, I never wanted to spend another day of my life without her in it.

The End

Want more of John and Ida? Stay tuned for "Legends Reborn"

This Soldier's Heart

Never Knew Goodbye
Jamie Summer

Prologue

I stared out at the water. The constant sound of waves crashing ashore was a companion I had long gotten used to. I'd always loved the ocean, but within the last few months, it had become a place I avoided at all costs. So, what brought me here today? I wasn't sure. I tried to come up with reasons today was different than any of the previous ones.

I had no idea.

It was hard to imagine it was merely three months ago. It felt more like a lifetime. My heart ached, the pain still as fresh as if he had left just hours earlier.

A dog barked, and I saw one of the few leftover tourists strolling along the beach. I had seen her and the golden retriever before. The animal happily trotted over to where I had taken up a position in the sand.

"Hey, buddy." He wagged his tail as I stroked his fur. His owner smiled at me as she walked by, then called out for him to follow. The dog barked at me, as if saying goodbye, before doing as he was told.

I watched them go, my heart heavy at the sight of the pair. It reminded me of the day I had been at this very beach. The day that changed my life.

I still wasn't sure if it had been for the best, and I contemplated that more than I should each day. Part of me knew the ending was inevitable, under circumstances I hadn't been privy to at the time, yet waking up that day and finding them gone had broken my heart into a million pieces. Each of them had anchored themselves in my mind, breaking loose painful memories I couldn't bear most days.

Falling in love with US Army Staff Sergeant Neil Brennan hadn't been part of my life's plan. After seeing what it had done to my parents, I didn't want to fall for a military man, but life didn't always go according to plan. I should know.

So, when I met a handsome, brown-haired guy at the beach one day, I knew life had decided to screw me over yet again.

Anthology

Chapter One

Amber

    The warm morning I woke up to wasn't unusual for this time of year. I felt my nightshirt sticking to my skin, a clear sign of the humidity in the air. It was one of the few things I didn't like about living in Virginia. Even in early fall, it could get incredibly hot and humid, a combination I wasn't very fond of.

    Groggy, I swung my legs out of bed and made my way over to the small kitchen of my apartment. The place I had rented almost a year ago was a tiny one-bedroom with a minuscule kitchen and small bathroom. However, it was mine, and that was all that mattered.

    The coffee maker, one of the first things I had bought after I moved in, was already brewing, thanks to the timer, so my morning fix wouldn't have to wait too long. I reached into the refrigerator and grabbed the milk, then opened the cupboard for a cup right when a beep announced the coffee was finished. I poured the black liquid and added milk...yes, I put more milk in than coffee...almost downing half of it on my first sip.

    I wasn't due at work for another two hours, so just like every morning, I decided to take a swim. The ocean was only a five-minute walk from my apartment, which was a definite selling point when I rented it.

    After placing my cup in the sink, I walked back into the living room. I put on my bathing suit, then a light sundress over it, knowing I needed something easy to take off and put on if I planned to do my usual morning round.

    I grabbed a towel from the bathroom and stuffed it into my small bag, grasped my keys and cell phone, and walked out the door. The humidity hit me in the face and I wiped my forehead, already feeling the first sweat droplets form.

Despite the humidity, I never planned on living anywhere else. I grew up around here and loved it. The people, the landscape, the ocean... It was perfect. It wasn't without its faults, but it was the right place for me. And with a job as a lead secretary for a huge law firm, I was able to stay in the area without any issues.

I followed the small sidewalks the city had built a few years ago. When I lived inland, I hadn't considered them worth our tax dollars, but now that I needed them, I was happy they were there. The small things in life.

As I rounded the corner, the sandy beach came into view. The sun, low on the horizon due to it being barely after six a.m., shone brightly across the surface of the water, illuminating every single wave rolling to shore. I walked toward where the shore met the ocean and took off my sandals.

As I took my first step toward the water, I heard a soft whine. I glanced around, trying to find the source, but I had a hard time making out anything in the bright sunshine. Hearing it again, I shielded my eyes from the sun in order to get a better look at my surroundings.

I spotted something in the sand a little farther down the beach. I wasn't sure what it was, but I started walking toward it. The noise got louder as I neared, making it clear I was heading in the right direction.

I saw a dog lying there in obvious pain.

"Hey, buddy. What's wrong?" I gently asked as I crouched down on the sand, putting my hand on its stomach. The golden retriever didn't show any outward sign of injuries, but the continued yelps made me think there had to be some kind of internal injury. I wasn't a doctor, but I had seen my fair share of *Chicago Med*.

Maybe he had been hit by a car? It was the only thing that made any kind of sense. There was a main street not far away, so he could have stumbled back to the beach.

"Max?! Max?!" a man called out. The dog's head slowly lifted and turned toward the sound. "Max?!"

I followed the dog's gaze. I saw a guy, dressed in boxers and putting on a shirt, standing outside one of the beach houses, looking around.

He spotted me before he did Max, but his steps quickened when he noticed his dog lying next to me.

"What happened? What did you do?" he asked. I was too perplexed to answer. "Did you hurt him? Think it's funny to hurt an animal?" He turned to Max. His hands, callused and tanned, stroked the dog's fur. Max's whines calmed down slightly.

"Excuse me, but I just came over to help. I heard your dog and wanted to see what was going on. Nothing else." I tried not to let the anger bubbling up inside me show, but it was hard when he had jumped to conclusions faster than I formed a thought.

His eyes, the golden color shining in the sunlight, pierced me with a stare. "You came over to help?" There was less anger behind the question this time, as if he realized his mistake.

I nodded, pointing to the street visible behind the houses. "I think he may have gotten hit by a car and came over here, but I didn't see anything."

He sighed. "Come on, big guy. Let's get you checked out," the guy said, not commenting on my remark.

More anger made its way through my pores. I came over to help, and this was the thanks I got?

He looked at me. "Thank you for checking on him."

He pulled Max into his arms and walked off. I heard muttered curses as he got about ten feet away. I knew I shouldn't listen, but I couldn't help myself. I leaned closer, trying to figure out what the issue was. Something about a car? Maybe a repair shop?

He turned around and met my gaze, indecision playing on his face. I waited, unsure of what he wanted. Shaking his head, his brown hair swaying, he sighed.

"Listen, I... I don't have a car here. It's at the shop. I hate to ask this, but is there any way you can drive us to the vet?" I stared at him in shock. "I know it's a lot to ask, so I understand if you have somewhere to be," he rambled. The nervousness in his voice, as well as the way he kept shooting worried glances at Max, made the decision easy for me.

I nodded. "I can take you." His eyes widened, obviously thinking I would deny his request. I wasn't sure if I should feel insulted or flattered, but went with the latter. "This way."

We walked toward the sidewalk. I quickened my steps, not wanting to waste a minute in case something was seriously wrong with Max. The dog continued to whimper, breaking my heart.

"I'm Amber," I said, feeling the need to say something to get his mind off his dog.

"Neil," he replied with a nod, then focused on the street in front of us.

It took less than three minutes to reach my building. I told Neil to wait outside while I ran up and changed. There was no way I would go anywhere looking like this. I knew it was slightly irrational, but I didn't want to show up at the veterinary office in my bathing suit. I quickly pulled on a pair of shorts and a tee, then ran downstairs again not even three minutes later.

Neil's brows were drawn together, and he bit his lips, his eyes barely leaving Max's body. He was worried for his companion, which made me want to speed through the city just to make sure we got the help he needed.

We entered the parking garage. "It's the white Mazda over there." I unlocked the doors and opened the back one, then grabbed an old blanket I had in the trunk and spread it out. Neil put Max on it before taking a seat beside him. I wasn't surprised he opted to take the back seat rather than sit in the front with me. I would have done the same.

I got in and started the car. I looked in the rearview mirror. "Do you know where the closest vet is?" When Neil nodded, I drove off. He directed me toward town, having me stop before we got into the city center of Norfolk.

He pointed. "It's over there."

I looked and saw the sign, a dog and cat on it. There was a parking lot right next to it. I turned into the small entrance, taking the first empty spot I saw.

It was early, but I hoped we could catch someone in the office already.

Neil jumped out of the car and quickly walked around, opening Max's door. The poor dog hadn't made any sound in a while, and I wasn't sure if that were a good sign or not. Worry gripped me as I watched him take Max into his arms, the dog not moving. Neil's forehead creased. I wanted to reach out and comfort him, a gesture I thankfully didn't follow through with.

He quickly made his way over to the entrance. I had a hard time keeping up with him, his legs longer than mine. When I saw the light on inside, relief washed through me.

Neil pushed through the door. "My dog is hurt. Is there anyone who can check on him?" I entered the waiting room right behind him, following him to the reception desk. "Please. I have no idea what's wrong with him, but he hasn't made a sound in over three minutes. I just..." He stopped. I saw a single tear slide down his cheek. He shook his head. The sight of this man so full of worry for the animal in his arms tugged at my heart. There had to be a history there, and I found myself wanting to know it.

"Sure, Mr...?"

"Brennan. Neil Brennan."

The woman in front of him took out a notepad and scribbled something down.

"Okay, Mr. Brennan. If you just fill this out, we'll get to the big guy right away." Her green eyes were filled with warmth as she came around the counter, pushing a gurney. I instantly felt myself reacting to her, knowing the dog would be in good hands. Neil seemed to come to the same conclusion because he put Max down on the gurney and took the clipboard she held out. He gave the dog another glance before the woman pushed the gurney into the back. With a heavy sigh, Neil focused on the papers in front of him. I had no idea what I was supposed to do, so I took a seat on one of the white plastic chairs in the waiting area.

Neil stayed rooted to the spot, apparently perfectly content with where he was. There were two other people waiting—a cat and another dog owner, both caught up in their own private conversations. I watched them for a while before I felt my stomach start to churn. I hated just sitting around.

I reached into my pocket for my phone and got up, calling work and telling them I'd be in a little later. I didn't have a set time I had to be there, as long as the work got done. I was required to be there a certain number of hours, but whether I did them with an early or late start was completely up to me. I hung up just as the woman came back out. Neil handed the clipboard back to her.

"Okay, we have him in back. Let me take you to a room so the doctor can talk to you."

Neil nodded. "Let's go." He started to walk off when he stopped mid-step. He turned his head, his eyes meeting mine. I could see the indecision written all over his face.

I smiled. "I'll wait out here."

He merely nodded before following the woman to the examination room.

Chapter Two

Neil

I walked after her as she stepped into a room to our right. There was a table in the middle, a computer sitting on it. An elderly lady stood next to it. She looked up as we entered, the other woman handing her my paperwork. Was she the same one who had greeted us? I wasn't sure anymore. All I could think about was Max.

"Good morning, Mr..." The doctor looked down at the clipboard. "Brennan." I nodded. "I'm Dr. Jerrit. We'll try to figure out what is wrong with Max. I see here that you're unsure of what happened?"

"I woke up and found him gone. He can roam freely because he never ventures far. I found him lying on the beach, but have no idea how he got there."

The doctor watched me, probably assessing how much of the story was the truth or whether I was an animal abuser.

I couldn't stand when animals were hurt. Eight years ago, I had saved Max from the animal shelter down the street from where I grew up, and he'd been with me ever since.

"Well, from what you put down, you think he may have been hit by a car?"

"When I found Max, there was a woman with him. She thought that's what could've happened."

"Very plausible," the doctor replied. "I'm going to do some x-rays. If there are internal injuries, it's important we catch them now. Why don't you take a seat while I go examine Max, then I'll come back in and explain what I found."

Nodding, I sat down as she left. Worry for Max flooded my mind the same way anger, relief, and apprehension did.

When was the last time I felt this restless? This worried about someone I cared about?

My hands felt clammy, so I wiped them on my shorts, only then realizing I hadn't bothered to get dressed. I was almost naked. Maybe I should have been embarrassed about it, but I couldn't care less.

Around twenty minutes later, the door opened, the doctor walking in. "All right. So, it looks as if there are no internal injuries. He seems to have a broken rib and a few bruises along his torso. More than likely, he was hit by a car, but it's not too serious. He needs rest, but that's about all. We'll send you home with some pain meds, just in case he seems uncomfortable."

Relief coursed through me, a feeling I reveled in for a moment before I let the smile spread over my face. "Seriously?"

She gave me a soft smile. "Yes. He'll be back to his old self in no time. I would suggest you take him home, let him rest, and make sure he has everything he needs within a few feet of him. He can go out briefly to relieve himself, but shouldn't go on any long walks for the next two weeks."

"Okay." I had no issues with that. We had a park close by, as well as the beach, which was plenty enough for Max to be happy about.

She gave me a few more tips on how to get Max back to full health and told me to come back in a few days if he wasn't getting better. She said she'd bring him up to me, so I left the room and walked into the reception area. I stopped to pay with the money Amber handed to me earlier already for this occasion, then saw the woman in question sitting right where I had left her. I didn't have time to really look at her earlier, too consumed by fear for Max.

Her long, blonde hair fell off her shoulders in waves, and the blue-green color of her eyes reminded me of the ocean. She had on shorts and a loose t-shirt, the casual appearance making her look sexy, yet not over the top.

I had debated taking her with me when I went into the room, but she was a stranger in every sense of the word. She had just been in the wrong place at the wrong time.

The right place and right time, my mind provided, but I pushed the thought down.

Upon seeing me, she jumped up and rushed over. "Is he okay?"

"Yes. A broken rib and a few bruises, but other than that, he'll be okay. It looks like your guess about him being hit by a car was right." She breathed out an obvious sigh of relief, which confused me. I tilted my head. "Why do you care so much? You only met him not even an hour ago."

Her face contorted slightly, and I wondered if my words were the reason. "It doesn't matter if I have known him for half an hour or half my life. I would never want anyone to hurt something that can't defend itself." There was a certain conviction in her voice that made me refrain from pointing out that Max was a big enough dog that he absolutely could defend himself...just not against a car.

"Okay. Well, thank you. Again."

She stared at me, the green hue around her eyes getting bigger the longer I held her gaze. There was something vulnerable about the way she watched me. I felt the protective part of my being, the one I had long buried within the deepest part of my soul, react to it.

"Here's our big man," the technician interrupted, bringing Max over on a leash. He walked slowly, but looked better than he had before we got here. I took the leash from her, breaking whatever moment Amber and I had. "Here are his pain meds, directions on the bottle. Take care, Max." She smiled and walked off.

"Shall we?" Amber asked. Without waiting for a reply, she walked over to the door and pushed it open. I picked Max up before I followed.

After I told Amber what the doctor said, we quickly ran out of topics to talk about, so we drove back in silence. There were so many things I wanted to ask, yet I couldn't bring myself to.

She's a stranger, nothing more. Nobody I should care about, no matter how she treated Max...or the way she glanced at me when she thought I wasn't looking, as if I were a puzzle she wanted to figure out.

No. Stop it, Neil.

More of those wayward thoughts entered my mind. I had gotten good at talking myself out of things that could potentially make my life better. After Lyn, I stopped going after things I wanted. I couldn't deal with the heartache another time.

She parked her car by my house and the two of us got out. I lifted Max and carried him over to the door. Amber followed, but stopped once we reached the threshold.

"Thank you. I appreciate you helping us out." It was a formal declaration, but all I was able to give her.

"You're welcome. I hope Max gets better soon," she replied with the same formality, then walked back to her car, giving me a small wave. I watched her get in and drive off, hoping I hadn't made a mistake.

Max lifted his head slightly, looking at the door. I smiled. "Liked her, did you?" He gave me a look, as if letting me know he knew exactly what was going on in my mind. It would be great if he could share it with me because I had no idea how to detangle the mess inside my head half the time.

I put him down on his dog bed while I got some fresh water and a treat for him. Max didn't move, perfectly happy with nuzzling the blanket next to him.

His whole demeanor seemed to be better, which led me to hope the doctor was right and he'd be up and running in no time. Even though she said two weeks of rest, I knew my dog. If he was feeling better, I'd have a hard time stopping him.

Good thing I had the next three weeks off. My first vacation in almost two years.

Guess it was me and the dog.

What a life.

Chapter Three

Amber

As I worked, I thought about Max and Neil. How were they doing? Was Max okay?

I stared at my phone, which was completely irrational since Neil didn't have my number. Even if he did, there wasn't any reason for him to call. About halfway through the day, I decided I'd stop by their place on my way home.

It's merely to check on Max. I needed to see he was okay with my own two eyes. It didn't have anything to do with his brown-haired, blue-eyed owner.

After I clocked out, I grabbed a pizza for dinner and drove to Neil's place. I knew it was a crazy idea, even thinking he'd close the door in my face once he caught sight of me, but when I rang the doorbell, he opened it with a soft smile.

"Hey," he said. "Didn't expect to see you again." I didn't blame him. I had absolutely no reason to be here.

"I wanted to check on Max and brought dinner...in case you're hungry." I held out the pizza box. The smile on his face widened. It made me feel less stupid about my impromptu visit.

"Actually, I haven't eaten all day." He stepped aside to let me in. The house was small and cozy. The outside, which was painted white, didn't look like anything special, but the inside had an old-school feel and was clean and organized, which surprised me.

Looking around, I saw Max lying in a dog bed in between the living room and the kitchen, not moving when I walked in.

"He just fell asleep. He's doing better, but tired. I don't think I've ever seen him sleep this much," Neil explained while making his way over to the open kitchen, which was separated from the living room by a counter. He put the pizza down.

"I'm glad he's doing okay." I glanced between the man in front of me and the dog he so deeply cared for.

"Me, too. I try not to think about what could've happened to him. I mean, if he were really hit by a car, it could've been so much worse."

I nodded. Max had definitely gotten lucky.

I watched as Neil got out two plates and cutlery, though I was unsure as to why he would need a fork and knife for pizza.

He asked me about myself. What I did for a living, where I was from... All things you wanted to know about a person you just met. All the things we hadn't touched on earlier when neither of us knew if we would see the other again.

I answered his questions as we sat on the barstools at the counter. Neil was so easy to talk to, I found myself lost in our conversation. It was the most random stuff, too. About how we both liked the ocean and how the sand felt between our toes. How we enjoyed doing nothing at home. How we found small pleasure in watching people. He was attentive when I talked, and I felt as if he soaked up everything I told him about myself. It was nice. While I tried hard to ignore it at first, I eventually let the flutter in my stomach come through. I didn't lead an exciting life by far, but Neil made me feel as if I did.

After dinner, we settled on the couch, a bottle of wine on the coffee table. Neil made sure I felt at home, asking me more than once if I needed anything.

At some point, Max joined us in the living room, taking up a spot on the floor next to Neil. The love and trust those two shared was clearly visible. Part of me envied their connection. It had been a while since I felt like that...with both human and animal. We used to have a cat growing up, but he and I never got along.

We went from one thing to another, always able to find something else to talk about. After the silence in the car this morning, I hadn't been sure whether we would be able to talk, but this night proved my worries were for nothing.

Our conversation soon turned to favorite movies.

"What? That's definitely not the best movie of all time. *It* is the best movie," Neil explained.

"*It?* The horror movie? I'm sorry. We can't be friends. No way will I ever watch a horror movie with you." I shuddered, the mere thought creeping me out.

Neil laughed. "Not a fan, I take it."

I shook my head. "Horror movies are the last thing I would ever watch. I'm such a scaredy-cat when it comes to those."

An image of Neil and me on this very couch, me cuddled into him, flashed in front of me. Heat crept up my cheeks. I got up, hoping to hide it from him. I walked over to the shelves and studied the picture frames sitting there. There were four. Three pictures with an older couple, probably his parents, and one with him and a woman.

"My parents. They died in a car accident two years ago." Neil's voice came from behind me. I spun around, coming face to face with his chest. I glanced up, his closeness making my throat dry up.

"I'm so sorry."

He nodded, and I saw the pain in his eyes at the memory of them.

"I can't imagine what that feels like."

"It's still hard. Losing them both due to something so stupid makes it even worse." He sighed. "They were on the highway and got caught in the middle of a street race. One of the guys lost control and hit my parents head-on."

My heart got heavier with every word he said. I felt a tear slip down my cheek. To my surprise, Neil reached out and wiped it away, his thumb lingering on my skin a little longer than necessary. His eyes never left my face, and I felt my heart unable to distinguish between the anguish at Neil's heartache and the irrational excitement at having him so close to me.

"I should go," I whispered.

He nodded, stepping back. "Okay," he replied. "I want to go out with Max tomorrow morning for a bit. If you want to, you're welcome to come with us."

Despite the war of feelings raging in my heart, I felt myself nod. "I'd love that." I slowly put on my coat and shoes. Neil waited, Max by his side, both watching me carefully.

"Goodnight, Amber," Neil whispered as I reached for the doorknob. He gave me a chaste kiss on the cheek, and I felt his touch linger long after I left.

As I drove home, I realized I still knew nothing about Neil's life. I knew his likes and dislikes, but didn't know anything about where he came from or what he did for a living. He had managed to make this night about me. While I felt the flutter in my stomach at the thought, I made a note to ask him about it. I wanted to know everything there was to know about Neil Brennan.

Everything.

Chapter Four

Neil

I woke up the next day when I felt a wet nose in my face. As I opened my eyes, Max's face was right in front of mine. He barked the moment he noticed he had my attention, a clear sign he wanted to go outside. He apparently felt a lot better already.

Amber.

I remembered we'd agreed to meet up this morning. Excitement rushed through me, quickly followed by dread. I shouldn't become attached. She didn't deserve it, and I told myself I didn't, either.

I had purposely avoided all talk about my profession the night before. I focused the conversation on her, and while I loved to hear about what made her tick, it was also a ruse to stop her from asking questions about my life. Questions I couldn't answer.

There were times I hated the job I chose. I loved serving my country and knew I was doing good, but the more I was sent on missions—never knowing when or if I would return—the less I remembered what being home felt like. Having three weeks off was a rarity...although it had been forced on me, just like after my parents died.

My life had always been about the job. Until I met Lyn.

I shook my head, the sight of her bloodied body ingrained in my memory unlike anything else. It was my fault she was dead. They always said death was a necessary evil when it came to the job. Well, none of them had lost the person they wanted to spend the rest of their life with.

I swallowed back the anger and focused on Max staring at me expectantly. I got up and walked to the bathroom, taking a shower. It was shortly after seven, so I had about ten minutes. Amber had mentioned she needed to be at work around eight thirty, so we would have an hour before she needed to leave. Enough time for Max to get some fresh air. At least that was what I told myself.

Lyn. I have to remember Lyn.

Once I was ready, I glanced out the window and saw Amber strolling along the beach in our direction.

"Ready?" I asked Max. He barked in response. I opened the door and he trotted outside, right toward Amber. It seemed my dog took as much a liking to the beautiful blonde as I did.

She wore dark jeans and a floral top, which was a different look than the day before, but no less sexy. The pants hugged her curves, and the top accentuated every line of her body.

Lyn.

Lyn.

I repeated the mantra in my head, reminding myself of the ugly life I led that Amber didn't deserve to be subjected to...no matter how much I was beginning to want her to be. I didn't want to taint her light with the darkness buried deep within me.

"Morning," she greeted me with a smile. She held her flip-flops, walking along the sandy beach in her bare feet.

"Good morning," I replied, but the smile I wanted to show her didn't appear. Amber's smile faded, and she turned away from me, staring out at the ocean. It had already started. The way I managed to push people away before they got too close. Before I let myself care too much.

"Hey, Max," she said, bending down to stroke his fur. When he nuzzled her hand, she smiled in response, cuddling his head. If Max could grin, I was pretty sure he would. He loved the attention. "Glad to see you walking around." I was content to watch the two while I stood on the sidelines. It was a position I had no one to blame for but myself.

"Do you want to walk a bit?" I finally asked, hoping to convey some sort of happiness at her being here. Amber's eyes, filled with a mixture of apprehension and sadness, met mine.

"Sure. Do you think Max is up for it?" she asked.

I nodded, smirking. "He woke me up this morning with a wet nose. He wants to be out here."

A slow smile spread across Amber's face. I found myself looking forward to her showing it off, hoping it'd be directed at me one day, instead of my furry friend.

Jesus, what was I doing? I knew nothing could ever become of this, yet I allowed myself the pleasure of her company. Why? It was all kinds of messed up. I was taught better than that. My mom told me to never lead a girl on. It wasn't fair to anyone's heart. There were lots of other things my mom had told me, most of which I got very good at ignoring.

Max's sandy paw landed on Amber's jeans before I could react. "Max, no. I'm so sorry," I apologized.

She waved me off. "No worries. I kinda like the excitement." The sincere smile, now directed at me, made my breath falter for a moment.

Shaking the unnecessary notion off, I motioned to the beach. "Walk?" I asked again because we still hadn't moved. She nodded.

We started our stroll along the ocean, the gentle crash of the waves our only companion. I liked the silence between us this time around. Nothing was forced, as if we were both content with nature's sounds. Max walked in front of us, next to us, behind us. He changed positions as he saw fit. Nothing was left of the injured dog I picked up yesterday.

Two weeks, my ass.

"He seems to be doing much better," Amber commented, as if knowing exactly where my mind had gone. Or maybe she simply noticed the way I had been watching Max the past few minutes, making sure his small limp wasn't anything to worry about.

"He is. He's not completely back to normal yet, but seeing him walking around, being excited and happy, is more than enough right now."

"I can imagine. Seeing him yesterday, I didn't expect him to be able to run along the shore," she said, her voice small, yet sincere.

"Same here. But that's Max. A fighter."

"And you? Are you a fighter, too?"

Such a loaded question. I couldn't answer her figuratively. I also couldn't tell her about the things I had done, the people I killed in the name of my country. I couldn't.

"I would like to think so. I fought for this house. The owner wasn't gonna give it to me because of Max, but I convinced him, introducing them. How could he *not* give me the house after that?" I grinned. Amber laughed at my weak attempt at a joke.

"What else are you, Neil Brennan?" Her words were conversational, merely curious, but with every bit of myself I gave to her also came the possibility she'd crack me open. Something I had avoided letting someone do for a long time.

"Boring. Normal. But breathtakingly handsome, of course." Again, that smile.

She turned her head toward the ocean, her expression pensive. I watched her, memorizing the lines of her neck, the sweet spot behind her ear, the small dimple on her cheek. I wanted to reach out and touch her, explore if her hair was as soft as it looked, if the skin peeking out from her collar was as tempting to touch as it was to stare at, but I refrained.

I couldn't.

I never could.

Chapter Five

Amber

We continued to walk along the beach for another half an hour before I told him I needed to head back. It was an interesting and charming walk, more entertaining than I thought Neil gave himself credit for. He made me laugh and roll my eyes, at the same time being surprised by the stories he told. He had traveled the world and didn't shy away from sharing some of his memories, no matter if they were funny, sad, or downright outrageous.

Yet, through all the jokes, he was never quite able to get rid of the single speck of darkness in his eyes. He tried it hide it, but after living a life around people who always lied to me, I could read the signs. I tried not to let it get to me, telling myself it was only the second time the two of us had an actual conversation. If there were any demons haunting him, there was no need for me to feel insulted about not having learned about them yet.

Once we got back to his place, Max gave me a sloppy kiss before trotting off toward the house. Neil watched me, the darkness in his blue eyes making me wonder if I wasn't the only one who didn't want the morning to end.

"I need to get to work, but maybe we can get together again sometime soon," I said, hoping I didn't read him wrong.

"Same time tomorrow?" Neil asked. My heart skipped a beat.

"Yes," I breathed out. He smiled, then turned and followed Max to the house.

I watched the two disappear before I headed home. Seeing as I had packed everything in my car before leaving for the beach, I walked into the garage instead of going upstairs.

Ten minutes later, I was at work, questions being fired at me the moment I entered. I answered them the best I could, then found solace and quiet in my office. Jen, my best friend and co-worker, came in five minutes later, a steaming cup in her hand.

"Please, tell me that's coffee," I said. She nodded. Due to my early morning date, I had only gotten one cup of coffee in. That was not nearly enough to get me through the day. When Jen put the cup in my hand, I inhaled deeply.

"So, what's going on with you?" she asked, looking at her nails. It was a clear sign she was dying to ask me something, but didn't want to appear too nosy.

"Everything's great. What about you?" I replied. Not giving her what she wanted was way too much fun for me to pass on.

"Good, good."

Silence spread as I sipped my coffee.

"What have you been up to lately? I haven't talked to you in ages."

Another lame attempt at getting information out of me. I had no idea what she wanted me to say, but it was clear she waited for something. Plus, I had just seen her the day before. We had lunch together, so it had hardly been ages.

"Not much. You know me and my boring life."

"So, no early morning veterinary visits?"

My eyes bulged, shock rippling through me. It wasn't that I had meant to keep it secret, but I had no idea what this thing with Neil was to start with. Having her put me on the spot made me nervous. And itchy.

"How do you know about that?"

"Ha! So, you *have* been doing dirty deeds," Jen exclaimed. I rolled my eyes at her dramatics.

"I have done no such thing. I merely helped out a dog in need, nothing else."

"I heard he was good-looking."

"The dog? Yes, Max is cute." She gave me a pointed look. "Not what you were talking about?" I innocently asked.

"Tell me everything," she demanded, so I did. After all, she was my best friend. There wasn't much to tell anyway.

"So, we spent this morning at the beach, talking, laughing. It was nice," I concluded.

"Just nice? Or *really* nice?"

I shrugged. I liked Neil, liked being with him, but I couldn't deny the barrier he'd built between us.

"I have a feeling there's something he's not telling me," I admitted.

Jen nodded thoughtfully. "Maybe it isn't meant for you to know yet. I know it's hard, especially when you start out, but sharing deep, possibly dark secrets with someone takes time. You've known him what... Two days? Hardly enough time to warrant that."

She was right. I hadn't earned the right to know his secrets. But I wanted to. I wanted him to trust me enough to tell me everything about him, even the parts he was afraid to show.

"We agreed to meet again tomorrow morning."

"A daily date?" Jen smirked. "I like it. And he sounds like a great guy. Plus, anyone who cares about a dog the way it sounds like he does has to care for his female companion the same way. Even more so." Though the comparison left a bit to be desired, I knew what she was trying to say. "I know you're hesitant, but for once, why don't you try to leap instead of slowly climbing down? There may be someone there to catch you."

I sighed. It wasn't like me. I wasn't the kind of person who'd run into a relationship. I was careful. Hesitant. Exactly as Jen said. With Neil, things were different. He made me want to be braver. More reckless. He made me consider jumping for the first time in my life.

"Thank you," I whispered.

"Don't thank me yet. Thank me once you've shared his bed and he's declared his undying love for you." She laughed, and I couldn't stop my eye roll. The buzzer on my phone went off and Liz, my fellow secretary, told me the bosses wanted to see me. "That's my cue. Take the plunge, woman, and don't be afraid to fall."

With that, Jen walked out, leaving me alone, my thoughts revolving around the brown-haired man I couldn't get out of my head.

Chapter Six

Neil

After Amber left, Max and I spent the day lounging on the couch, walking a little more around the park or the beach, and eating. It was the perfect vacation.

There was a small part of me that wished Amber were here to do it all with us. I knew Max liked her and wouldn't mind, and I found myself wondering how it would be to spend a whole day with her. I cursed myself. There was no way I was going down that road again. My mind had a different opinion on the matter, though. The more I tried to forget about Amber, the more images of her popped up.

Obviously sensing my tumultuous state, Max tried to keep me busy with entertaining him. He limped a bit, but nothing that worried me too much. So, we played whatever my dog wanted. As long as he was happy, I was, too.

Almost.

As the night neared, I made dinner, tempted to go over to Amber's and invite her. Cooking wasn't something I usually did for myself, but I had done so with her in mind. Max didn't complain, since he got to share my food. Afterward, we settled on the couch. Max fell asleep before long, his heavy and even breathing the only sound echoing along the walls.

I couldn't take the silence and turned on the TV. It didn't matter what was on. I needed some kind of distraction. I flipped through the channels and got stuck on a cheesy movie love story. My finger hovered over the remote more than once, but I couldn't bring myself to change it. I was caught up in this story about a man falling in love with the woman of his dreams. It was way too girly for me, but somewhere in the back of my mind, I wanted to be him. I wanted to have the happy ending I had no doubt he'd get.

I wasn't worthy of a happy ending.

After several hours, I turned off the TV. Not only had I finished watching the romantic movie, but also watched a second one. Lyn had always loved those kinds of movies. She hadn't forced me to watch them, but I always did. It made her happy, so I wanted to be able to share it with her. And if it got to be too much, there was always a good book that would keep me busy.

Lyn.

The pain, which was a constant ache a few days ago, had lessened noticeably. I tried not to think too much about the reasons for it, but it was difficult. Amber was different than Lyn. Whereas Lyn was outgoing, loud, always the center of attention, Amber was shy and quiet. However, once you got her to talk, the light in her eyes showed her passion for the things she shared with you. Seeing the love for life reflected in her eyes was a trait I treasured immensely.

I let my head fall back against the pillows of the couch, sighing deeply. Why couldn't it be morning already?

I got up. If I wanted to be somewhat awake tomorrow when Amber came over, I knew it was time for me to go to sleep.

♥

I must've fallen asleep instantly because Max's bark was the next thing I heard. Sunlight streamed through the floor-length windows, bathing my bedroom in a gorgeous morning glow. Before I was able to admire it, Max barked again...but he wasn't in the room with me. Instantly on high alert, I threw on my jeans and a shirt before rushing over to the hallway. My dog sat by the door, his eyes focused on it.

"What is it, Max?" He barely gave me a glance before focusing on the door again. The clock on the wall read shortly after six a.m. It was too early for Amber, wasn't it? I grabbed the handle and flung it open, ready for any fight waiting for me. Pleasant surprise warmed me at the sight standing there.

She jumped. "Hey. I'm so sorry. I woke you, didn't I?" I saw a blush working its way over her cheeks.

"Yes, you did," I replied, but before I could tell her it was all right, she continued.

"Oh shit, I'm sorry. I just... I couldn't sleep, so I decided to take a walk on the beach. When glanced over and saw Max already up, standing at the window, I thought you might be, as well. Stupid. I'll leave and come back later." She spun around and started to walk off.

I reached out, grasping her arm. "Wait." I didn't want her to go. "Would you like some coffee?"

Indecision flickered across her face. "Okay." It was a quiet, unsure answer, but was all I needed for my heart to skip a beat. I opened the door wider. She walked in, Max on her in an instant. I smirked. "I'm beginning to think he likes you better than me."

She smiled up at me as she stroked his head. "He doesn't see me as much as you. Plus, I'm the new, shiny toy he gets to play with." It seemed it only took a second with Max for all her worries to disappear. Could I be jealous of the connection my dog had with someone? Jesus, what was wrong with me?

"All right... Coffee," I said, more to myself than her.

I crossed the hallway and entered the kitchen. As I got everything ready, I heard soft footsteps, as well as Max's paws, crossing the wooden floor.

"Was there a reason you couldn't sleep?" I asked, my back toward Amber. If there were any nightmares plaguing her, I wanted to know about it.

"No, not really. I came home late from work last night and always have trouble sleeping when that happens.

It seems going to bed early gives me a more restful sleep than going to bed late."

"Isn't that a natural thing?" I smiled, looking over my shoulder at her.

"You would think so. However, it didn't used to work like that for me. It was the other way around. Going to bed at ten p.m. would have me tossing and turning, whereas going to bed later had me feeling more energetic than ever the next morning."

I nodded, intrigued. "I'm like that. I work best at night and can't handle mornings."

Amber arched a brow. "You look fine to me," she said.

I knew it was a statement in reply to my comment, but I couldn't help the once-over I gave myself. I had grabbed the first jeans and shirt I had seen, not even sure they were clean.

"Thanks," I replied, a cough masking the slight embarrassment working its way through me. I faced Amber, watching as she took a seat on one of the barstools. I joined her.

"I'm glad you stopped by earlier than we agreed." The words were out before I could stop them, and I wanted to take them back instantly. I'd known this woman all of three days. The last thing I wanted was for her to think me a creep.

"Me, too. I'm sorry about waking you, though."

"No need to be. I wanted to get up a little earlier anyway, so you came right on time." My eyes held hers. Her cheeks turned red. I didn't know if it was from the attention I gave her—or had wanted to give her—or something else.

"What do you think—" Amber started, but I didn't let her finish. Instead, I grabbed her face in my hands and kissed her.

Chapter Seven

Amber

I didn't see it coming, yet when Neil leaned forward to put his lips on mine, it was all I could think about. All I saw, felt, needed.

His kiss was light, gentle, testing, as if afraid of rejection, of pushing too far, too soon. I moved closer, letting him know I was perfectly okay with this. He deepened the kiss.

I let myself fall over the edge. The way Jen wanted me to. I stopped thinking about what-ifs and only cared about one thing...Neil.

He pulled away, resting his forehead on mine. "I'm..." He stopped. "Actually, no. I'm not sorry." A lazy smile crossed his lips.

"Neither am I," I replied hoarsely, knowing there was no part of me that regretted it. Quite the contrary. All I could think about was doing it again. His gaze went back to my mouth, letting me know I wasn't the only one.

He cleared his throat. "How about that coffee?"

I nodded, a stupid smile on my face. I cuddled into my black hoodie, hoping it would hide the giddiness I felt. A rush of energy flooded through me. I felt more alive than I had in days.

He put the coffee in front of me, then some milk and sugar. "I didn't know how you liked it, so I brought everything," he explained with a sheepish smile.

"Thank you." He sat down next to me again, a little closer this time. Our legs touched as we sipped our coffee.

Neil asked me about work the previous day, and I told him why I had gotten home so late. There wasn't anything besides indecisive bosses, but it was enough to keep me busy into the late hours. He listened patiently, asking questions here and there, making it clear he had an actual interest in the work I did.

"So, what do you do? For some reason, this has never come up, and I feel bad for not having asked before." At the question, the change in Neil was subtle, but it was there. He sat a little straighter, his shoulders a little stiffer, some of the lightness fading from his eyes.

"Boring office job, nothing else."

"Boring office job? That's all?" He nodded. I arched a brow at him. "That's not really an answer."

A tight smile played on his lips. "It's a boring office job in the military, just shuffling papers around."

My eyes widened. Considering we lived close to several military bases, I shouldn't have been surprised, yet I couldn't help the small stab of fear.

"The military?" I asked, as if I hadn't heard his answer.

"Yeah. Like I said, it sounds more glamorous than it actually is."

I took a deep breath, then nodded. "Okay."

"It's certainly not as exciting as clients storming in, yelling at me." He laughed, but it was strained. Forced. Hollow.

Why had the mere mention of his job turned his mood sour? I wanted to go back to when we kissed, when everything was about us connecting, not drifting apart.

"I'm sorry, Amber, but my job isn't something I like to talk about. It's boring, like I said, but there are also a lot of confidential things I can't talk about, even if I wanted to. I know it's not a very satisfying answer, but it's all I can give you." Neil's eyes met mine, willing me to believe him.

"I know the feeling," I replied, expecting the arched brow in question before I saw it.

"Do tell." Neil put his coffee down and turned his body toward me, giving me his full attention.

"There isn't much to tell. My parents both worked in the military, office jobs, until they were recruited for actual missions. Deadly ones. I rarely saw them as a child, or even as a teenager. I spent more time at my grandparents' house than at my own. I knew it was their dream job and they loved it, but I still hated never knowing where they were going, what they had to do. One day, a few days before they were scheduled to return, a man came to the door.

"My parents had died, but they couldn't tell us how. Top secret. Hearing your parents died is bad enough, but not knowing what happened to them is even worse. You always wonder if it's really true. If they actually *did* die." I gave a dry laugh. "It's really stupid because I know they are dead, but I couldn't help the feeling for a long time. Not even at the funeral." I wiped the tears I felt running down my cheek. I hadn't meant to start crying, but the memory still hurt.

I glanced up at Neil, seeing unshed tears in his own eyes. It surprised me. I had no idea what went on in his head, and wasn't sure I wanted to know. There was too much pain on his face. Too much to just be connected to my parents' deaths. Was it possible he lost someone else close to him in addition to his parents? I wanted to ask, but couldn't bring myself to. He would tell me once he was ready.

He grasped my hand under the table and squeezed it tightly, letting me know he was there for me. We sat like that for a long time as I remembered my parents as best I could.

I tried not to let his job cloud my excitement of being with him, but it had put a little damper on it. Now I had a small fear of him ending up the same way my parents had.

Office job. He only has an office job. I need to remember that.

Max strolled over to us from where he had taken up a spot by the window and nuzzled our legs with his nose.

"It seems someone wants to go out," Neil said, the smile back on his face. Some of the darkness had left his eyes, but I wanted to get rid of the rest, too. Maybe the walk would do just that.

I glanced out the window, seeing the sun shining brightly along the beach and across the water. A sight that never failed to amaze me.

"Ready?" Neil asked. I nodded, following the two outside. Whatever had happened to cause the shift, I prayed we could move past it.

Maybe even go back to what we were doing before things got so heavy.

Chapter Eight

Neil

The revelation about her parents should have made me run. It should have made me see how much I would eventually hurt her. The possibilities, the dangers my job could bring.

But I did nothing.

Instead, we spent the better part of the next three weeks together. We used every available moment we had—taking walks along the beach, going out to eat, the movies, the park, anything. Every second I didn't spend with her was torture.

Against my better judgment, I had fallen in love with her. And it had barely taken a breath of time.

By the time my vacation was over, Amber and I had talked about my job a few more times. I continued to omit the fact that a boring office job wasn't exactly all it entailed. While it was true I did paperwork, I knew I'd have another assignment soon. The danger would be inevitable...as would possible death.

I couldn't tell her. I didn't want it tainting the relationship we'd started to build over the past few weeks. So, I went to work each morning, telling her as little as I could at night.

It worked for a few weeks...until the assignment came up.

The day I was handed my next job was the day I needed to leave her. I knew it. The certainty within me didn't budge, no matter how much I wanted it to. I wanted to have more time with her. More cherished moments.

From the moment we met, I knew we were on borrowed time, but I had been the only one aware of it. I hadn't had the decency to fill Amber in, which I hated myself for.

When I came home that day, I found Max waiting by the door. Amber was supposed to come over for a home-cooked meal. I had promised her I'd whip up something special because it was our two-month anniversary. It wasn't a special number, but to us, it was reason to celebrate.

Now I had to ruin it all.

Sighing, I walked into to the kitchen and stored the groceries I had gotten for tonight's meal. Since I was leaving tomorrow, I didn't need anything else.

Just as I put the spaghetti into the water, the doorbell rang. I opened the door, wanting to kiss her hello, but Max pushed me to the side, demanding to be greeted first. Amber's laugh rang in my ears.

"Hello there." She smiled, leaning down to stroke Max for a good five minutes before straightening and turning her attention to me. "You think he'll be happy for the rest of the evening now?" she asked, pressing her body against mine.

"What did you have in mind?" I saw the dark desire in her eyes.

"Food." She moved past me and toward the kitchen. "This smells amazing," she commented and snuck a glance in the pots.

"Hands off. This is my workplace, so please, if you would be so kind..." I pushed her out of the immediate cooking area and placed her on one of the stools. She took off her jacket, placing it on the stool next to her. I watched her for a second longer before she pointed toward the sauce, which had started boiling over. I cursed and took it off the burner.

Fifteen minutes later, dinner was served. Amber couldn't stop complimenting me on it. I sat a little straighter and couldn't hide the pleased grin. I gave Max a little portion, as well, and Amber admonished me—not for the first time—for spoiling the dog with food not made for him.

After dinner, we cleared and washed the dishes, then got comfortable on the couch, where we had spent a lot of our hours together. We loved the same movies and never had any issue choosing one.

The credits of the action movie rolled on the screen way too fast. The more time passed, the more my panic flared. I still hadn't figured out how I'd tell Amber about needing to leave. Or if I even would. The thought of seeing the disappointment flash across her face was like a heavy, invisible burden on my shoulders. The faster the hands of the clock moved, the worse it got. Until it threatened to suffocate me.

"Are you okay?" she asked, worry in her eyes.

I squashed all the bad thoughts swirling in my head. I didn't need them clouding our last night together. I wanted us to enjoy whatever time we had left.

"I'm fine. Sorry," I assured her, reaching out to brush a strand of her blonde hair behind her ear. She leaned into the touch, and I kissed her gently. She moved her body to face me, but it wasn't nearly fast enough. I pulled her onto my lap. Our kisses became more frantic, her erratic breath mingling with my own. I slowed down, drawing out the pleasure of our kisses a little more.

"Tease," she complained, but I just hushed her with another kiss. My hands moved along her cheeks, down her neck, my fingertips playing with her skin. Soft moans escaped Amber's lips, the sound urging me on. She moved her hips on my lap, suddenly making my jeans feel tight. "Don't play too long," she whispered against my lips.

I smirked, picking her up. She put her legs around my waist, kissing every inch of my face, as I carried her to the bedroom.

"You're gonna make me fall," I admonished her as I almost stumbled over the small threshold leading to the bedroom.

"Shouldn't you be able to navigate your space blindly?"

When we reached the bed, I put her down on it, taking a moment to revel in the sight of her. She fit into my life so perfectly, the mere thought of forever erasing her out of it made me falter for a moment.

"I love you," I whispered for the first time as I bent down to claim her lips yet again. I didn't want her to say it back, but I knew she felt the same way. It was written all over her face, visible in everything she did. I just couldn't bear to hear the words.

As if she felt it, she merely nodded in response and intensified our kisses. I felt all the words I didn't want her to say in the way she kissed me, the way her hands roamed my body, and I treasured the moments I had with her. I peeled off her shirt and jeans, Amber an eager helper as she got me out of my own clothes. She touched every inch of skin she found, her erratic breath something I would never get used to. And wouldn't have the chance to.

I loved the fact she was so open with me. She didn't hold anything back. Not when I took off her bra and panties. Not when I let my hand glide between her legs, finding her more than ready for my touch. There was something empowering about seeing her reaction to every one of my movements. I teased her relentlessly, feeling her shiver under my hands. Her hooded eyes raked over my body, which made the need for her grow. Her long legs on my white sheets were perfect in this uncertain world I lived in.

I followed her, kissed her, loved her in every way possible. I didn't stop until both of us were out of breath and unable to move any longer. It was one of the sweetest feelings I had ever known.

When I had to leave the next morning, I knew I would never forget the way Amber looked that night. The happy smile on her lips, the way her eyes glossed over when she watched the starry night outside. The way her body fit perfectly with mine. The way I told her everything I wanted her to know.

Before everything came crashing down.

Epilogue

Amber

I passed by their house as I stumbled back to my apartment. Three months. It had been three months since I woke up in Neil's home...alone. At first, I didn't think anything of it. He could've been in the bathroom or in the kitchen, but the moment I got up and Max's bark didn't greet me, I knew something was wrong.

Thinking back on it now, panic seized me, the same way it did back then. I was barely able to breathe through the haze of tears forming in my eyes. I had searched every inch of the house, but there was nothing left of them. Most of Neil's clothes were gone, as were Max's things.

How had they managed it without waking me up? Where did they go? Would they be back? Maybe they had only gone out for a morning stroll.

While I had tried to tell myself there was a rational explanation for their absence, the pain in my chest knew there wasn't. It was as if my heart knew it would break before I did.

Wind blew, the icy cold reminding me the seasons were about to change. I pulled my jacket closer to my body as I unlocked the door to my apartment, the wind not the only thing making me shiver. I walked past the mirror in my hallway and stopped, seeing the silent tears I hadn't realized I'd been crying. I quickly wiped them away with my sleeve, not wanting another reminder of what I had lost.

I tried to forget about them. Tried everything I could to not linger on the way being with Neil made me feel.

Alive, free, reckless. Loved, safe, *home*.

My eyes fell on the small note next to my fireplace. It hadn't moved since I put it there three months ago. I couldn't bear to touch it again. It had been painful enough to find the house empty and devoid of the person I had come to love, but what I wasn't prepared for was what he wrote.

I had found it stuck in between the box of coffee and the coffee maker. Neil knew me well enough to know it was one of the first appliances I'd find myself drawn to, no matter if he were there or not. He was right.

The note was scribbled on the back of the receipt of one of his many pizza orders, but I didn't care. All I hoped when I found it was that it would be a few lines about having gone out to get breakfast or something.

It wasn't.

Dear Amber,

I sit beside you as I write these lines, but I already know I'm not going to be able to put everything into words. The amount of love I have for you can't be expressed on paper, no matter how much I try. There has not been a single moment I haven't wanted to be with you. The weeks we've had together were unlike anything I have ever experienced, and probably won't again. The joys, the laughs, the fun we had, even the tears... I enjoyed every second of it. I'll treasure everything in the deepest part of my broken heart.

I need to go. Although I know you won't understand, know that leaving is one of the hardest things I've ever had to do in my life.

I tried my best to keep away from you. I didn't do a very good job, but I knew getting attached to you would only lead to one thing—heartbreak. And it was the last thing I wanted you to go through.

I was selfish. I wanted you for myself, for however long I had. There was always an end date to our relationship. I just didn't know when it was going to be.

It was not fair to you, and I honestly hope part of you hates me for it. It's better than thinking you sit at home, waiting for me to come back.

Amber, I won't.

Not because I don't want to, but because I can't. Once I leave, there is no returning to the place I came from. Every time I start a new job, I vow to myself I will start anew somewhere completely different once I return. Whenever that will be. A month? A year? Ten? I don't know.

There were several blotches on the paper, as if tears had overwhelmed him while writing those lines.

Know that no part of me regrets being with you. The only regret I have is not having had enough time. Not a single moment was wasted. I love you, Amber. I did from the first moment you glanced up at me when you were kneeling next to Max on the sand. Thank you for reminding me what love can be like. How it can make you feel. Please, promise me one thing. Find it again. Find someone you can give your heart to who won't leave you. You deserve nothing less.

Forever,
Neil

My eyes welled up with tears. I didn't need to read the letter again to know what it said. I'd memorized every single line of it. More than once, I thought about burning it, but it would also burn the only tangible connection I had with him. Even now, I found myself wondering if there were a chance he might break his promise to himself. That he wouldn't start over somewhere else. That he'd come back here. The more time passed, though, the smaller my beacon of hope became.

I hated him for not telling me the truth. For knowing we were on limited time and not sharing it with me. There was, however, a part of me that understood. The time we had was carefree, without a black cloud hanging over us. I treasured every moment with him because that was the way I was raised to live my life.

Time was a precious thing, something you needed to cherish and handle with the utmost care. If you didn't, it would slip through your fingers before you realized it.

Time wasn't endless.

Time wasn't something we had in spades.

Time was a meter.
And ours had run out.

The End

This Soldier's Heart

Restless
Arielle Adams

And I lay wide awake
eyes clenched tight but sleep
is still a faraway concept

I'm thinking of you
and wondering when
you'll hold me in your arms again

how your chest will rise and fall
against my shoulders, your lips
tickling the back of my neck

how your hands will tangle with mine
resting over my breast, my heart
beating slow, lulling us both to rest

My love for you is limitless
I miss you more than words
as I wonder if you, too

find no peace tonight
I'm wondering if you
are thinking of me, too

This Soldier's Heart

A Soldier's Sunset
C.L. Foster & E.R. Rada

"Just leave me alone!" Shoving away from the wall, he thumped down into the wheelchair and started to roll away.

"Darren, you need this," the technician shouted as he tried to keep pace with the furious man in the chair.

"I don't need anything. I can do this myself." His pace quickened as he shot toward the nearest exit.

Cutting over the next turn, the tech jumped some stacked up mats and landed firmly in front of the wheelchair. Huffing, he said, "You're really fast in that thing, geez man."

Darren's eyes locked on the ground, his teeth gritting as his ragged breath huffed heavily.

"You are doing amazing. I know it's hard getting used to this change, but you're strong and—"

"Look, Phil," Darren cut him off. "I'm broken. Stop trying to fix me. Just let me go home and rot in peace."

"Nothing is ever broken, dude. We have duct tape and whatnot," he teased as he eased closer and slowly guided the chair to face back toward the workout wall. "Rotting is what dead things do and you're a survivor. Including a shiny new addition," he added, gesturing toward Darren's new prosthetic leg. "It's like you're a cyborg now.

We just have to teach you how to use that thing, that's all. I'm jealous. Do you know how long I've wanted to be part cyborg? I'm not brave enough to take the hit though."

A tight nod was all the man gave.

Leaning down, Phil lowered his voice. "You really are inspiring, soldier." If nothing else, the last week had shown him that using that one word often got Darren moving. "You sacrificed for us and we are so grateful for your service. Please let us give something back to you. This is such a small gesture and definitely not enough, but we are honored to give it, if you will allow us." When Darren didn't move a muscle, Phil added, "The boss is giving me hell about all of my overtime and I think maybe a different tactic might help you along. I'm going to tag Alex in for you, will that be okay with you, soldier?" Maybe the added reference would give him some much-needed ground. "Not that I'm abandoning you. If you want, I will gladly stay and have your six off the clock."

"No man can help the lone wolf," Darren huffed as he pulled himself up onto the rails and took a shaky step away from the wheelchair.

"That's because sometimes you need a woman's touch to fix a problem," Alex said as she stepped around the corner. She immediately leapt toward Darren as he toppled over from her surprise entrance. "Oh gosh, I'm really sorry. I was trying to make a smooth entrance. I guess I was a little scary looking or something. Or was it my breath? I did have Italian for lunch," she joked as she guided Darren back toward the rails.

"Excuse me, ma'am," he managed while hastily adjusting his stance, a new frown creasing his forehead as he averted his eyes. "I didn't hurt you, did I?"

She chuckled. "You have to try harder than that. I'm tough."

"Of course," he nodded. "I didn't mean to imply you are weak."

"Again, I'm tough," she assured. "Inside and out. Much like you." His eyes seemed to be locked on his newest appendage as the frown on his forehead threatened to cut his head in half.

Studying his face for a moment, Alex stepped away, leaned against the wall, and crossed her arms over her chest.

Darren took a slight, timid step forward. His white-knuckle grip on the rail made the wood groan.

"You wanna tell me how you ended up trying to be a super cool, peg-leg pirate, Darren?"

Anger flared in his eyes as he finally looked into Alex's. "Are you mocking me?" he raged.

She chuckled. "Not at all. I just wasn't sure what would get you to see I'm also a person. Sometimes humor breaks silence, other times it pushes a situation over the edge. I couldn't know which one I was dealing with until I tried. Sue me." She took a small breath and pushed off the wall. "Okay, that's enough of that, fella. Let's have a seat." When he hesitated, she pushed the wheelchair forward, bumping into the back of Darren's knee making him falter.

Shooting an irritated look over his shoulder, he frowned before releasing the rails and plopping down into the seat.

"See? That wasn't so hard. Sometimes climbing the mountain is the easy part. It's getting to it that's the hard part," she started as she turned the chair and went toward a wide expanse of windows. "I'm here to facilitate the prep work." When he stayed silent, she added, "Of course, if you'll allow that. As I prefer to come into a case on a clean slate, I haven't read any of your file. I don't know where you came from or what you did before this. I don't know how long you've been at this or what you need. All I know is I see determination in a kind looking face and I'd love to cheer you on while you climb the mountain." Parking in front of the window, she sat next to Darren's wheelchair on a cushioned stool. "See there?" she pointed toward the horizon as the sun began to dip. "I love watching the sunset. It's like a gift to me not only to let me know that my part of the day is done, but when she rests, I can rest. It seems silly, but I try to always give everything my best when the sun is watching me. She doesn't get a day off and neither do we."

Darren watched in silence as the sun continued setting. The gorgeous colors across the sky mesmerized them both until a buzzer went off in the background.

"Oops. Welp, that's your time. Tomorrow, same place?" she suggested as she stood to wheel him back toward the entrance.

"But I didn't give you any information to set up a workout plan for me or anything," he argued.

"I know my job and I'll be happy to show up every time the sun does. Don't worry."

"I wasn't worried, I--" he started, then stopped suddenly. "Okay, see you then."

"I'm Alexis, by the way, but my friends tend to call me Alex," she added, leaning down a bit to meet Darren's eyes again. Her hazel and gold eyes shimmered as she stretched her hand out to take his. "Nice to meet you."

"Same to you, ma'am. Darren, the pirate," he chuckled.

"Arrrrgh you?" she giggled.

"Are those puns part of my therapy? Cause if they will always be that bad, I will heal slower, I'm sure," he groaned, the tiniest of smiles pulled at the edges of his lips.

"No way, those are free of charge and just part of my charm. Make sure you eat a nice dinner and get lots of rest. I plan to kick your butt tomorrow. See you then!"

♥

The next day as Darren wheeled himself into the room, he saw Alex sitting on a medicine ball, next to the rails. "What have you planned for me today, ma'am?"

"You good at multitasking?"

"Arr," Darren grunted.

"Oh, now look who's the punny one!"

"Hmph, let's get on with this butt kicking of yours, shall we? The sun is still up, isn't it?"

"Very well, I want you to stand on both legs, shoulder width apart, at the edge of the rail and then toss me the medicine ball. Easy stuff," Alex directed, as she stood up, not offering him assistance.

Darren scowled at the whole idea, but didn't complain. He eased his way up out of his wheelchair, steadily shimmied his way from one end of the rails to the other, and set his feet shoulder width apart to steady himself the best he could.

Picking up the medicine ball, Alex looked to Darren. "Ready?"

He gave her a tight nod as his full body tightened to prepare for the blow.

With a light toss, Alex gave the ball to Darren who stumbled, but caught himself without falling. He steadied himself and tossed the ball back, a rigid grin threatening to cross his lips.

"Coquelicot," Alex said randomly as she tossed the ball again.

"Bless you?" Darren asked with a chuckle, catching with a thud that made him correct his stance again.

"It's my favorite color," Alex returned the ball with a brilliant smile.

"Ah, so we'll have small talk now?" When she didn't answer and kept up her tosses, Darren added, "I like poppies. Mine is blue. Any shade will do."

Visibly shocked by his color knowledge, Alex grinned. "Skydiving."

"I'll take Things I'd Never Do for $500, Alex," Darren grinned.

"It's on my bucket list, but I just don't really see the point of jumping out of a perfectly good airplane. Maybe if it were on fire or something, but I'd rather it land safely somewhere warm."

He nodded. "I feel similarly. I have jumped out of one, but because it was part of my training. I'd never do it for fun." She stayed silent for another throw, waiting for him to continue. "Cockroaches."

Alex snorted and nearly missed the ball Darren had tossed. Taking a moment to correct her own stance, she stared at him, her eyes twinkling with amusement. "Definitely Things I'd Never Do list," she said before taking a step back and relaunching the ball.

"I mean, it's on my bucket list to eat bugs, but it's not something I'm racing to do," he laughed.

"Who wants to eat bugs? On *purpose!*"

"Hey, it's a cultural thing. Don't knock it 'til you try it, ma'am."

Their silence stretched for a few more tosses with no falls before Darren glanced at the clock and realized half an hour had already passed and he was standing on his own, without the help of the rail at all. "What kind of madness is this? I've only been walking the rails for a few weeks! Now I'm throwing a ball and standing on my own. It doesn't even hurt."

"Comfort zones are for chumps," Alex smiled.

"You don't think coming here is getting out of my comfort zone in the first place?" Scowling, he tossed the ball a little too hard, making him stumble and catch himself on the rails for the first time during their session. "This whole place is outside my comfort zone."

"You can have comfort zones within uncomfortable places, too. Which is why I'm changing things up a bit. Like I said before, I didn't look at your file, but I took a guess on this. Chatting and doing something that seemed simple to you before is a good way to help you find your balance." She put the ball down and sat back on the ball. "Now tell me, what did you do in the military?"

Darren grunted at Alex's logic. "I was a sniper in the Marine Corp and did two tours in Afghanistan. I lost my leg to an IED while with a scouting party." He seemed to lose himself in thought as he leaned backward onto the railing. "It was an ordinary scouting trip, nothing special. Of course, they all are, right? My humvee hit an IED and shrapnel tore through the place like it was nothing. We didn't have time to think. Time to feel pain. Someone told me to move and I realized that I couldn't."

Alex watched his face contort from one emotion to another. The panic of being in the situation, the loss of brothers, the fear of not being able to move. "Yet your brothers never left your side. And you made it back to safety."

He wrinkled his forehead as his hand gripped the railing. "Not all of us made it back. We lost two good men that day. It wasn't just an IED, we took on fire. It was an ambush."

"You inspire me, to have gone through all that and to have the strength to keep moving forward like you do is truly awe inspiring."

Darren gave her a quick nod, his grip easing a bit on the wood. "What choice do I have? Live in the past and be haunted by my memories or keep moving forward. I choose life, even if I'd rather do things my way, on my own. That's what I'm used to. I'm a sniper, a lone wolf," Darren said with a grin.

"Well, Mr. Wolf, you need to follow training if you want to maximize your time here and heal as fast as possible. We don't want you limping around town like a pirate forever, do we?"

"Again with the pirate thing. I'm starting to think you have a thing for pirates."

"Well, maybe, beards are sexy and who doesn't like a bad boy?" Alex giggled. "Plus, pirates might seem hot, but their rum consumption is off the charts and you don't seem the type. Or I do I have you *pegged* all wrong?" she gestured to his leg with a wink.

Instead of taking her joke poorly, he groaned. "Really? Peg leg jokes?"

"It never stopped them from being badasses of the sea."

"Point well taken. Then, I shall grow a beard and call myself Pirate Pete, the scourge of the Atlantic Ocean!"

"Ha ha ha, are you trying to flirt with me?" A slight blush rushed her cheeks.

"Arrr."

A buzzer went off just as Alex stood. "Talk about timing. How's your leg doing?"

"It's probably going to be sore later, this was quite the workout. For now it feels oddly. . . strong."

"I told you I'd kick your butt today!" Smiling, she walked past Darren to head toward a storage cabinet. "So, I want to you have a seat and put on either a heating pad or ice pack, which would you prefer? Both will help, I'm leaving it up to you this time."

"Let's try the ice pack, see if that'll help."

"I'll set the timer for 15 minutes, after that you're free to head out. I have paperwork I must finish before heading out." She tossed the ice pack into his lap as he wheeled himself toward her favorite spot to watch the sunset. "I'll see you tomorrow then, yes?"

"Yep, I'm here 5 days a week. I'll see you tomorrow, ma'am."

♥

Days later, Darren wheeled himself up to Alex as she was talking to another worker. "Hey there, where have you been? I didn't see you the rest of last week. I thought you were going to kick my butt. Ran of out torture devices?" he teased.

Alex put on a fake smile as she turned to greet him, "Hey, Pirate Pete! Sorry, something came up last week and I had to deal with it. I promise to beat you up today." Her voice faltered at the end and he picked up on it right away.

"What happened? Are you ok?"

"I don't want to talk about it. It's personal." Alex started to walk toward the rails where the medicine balls were, but Darren cut her off. He didn't care about protocol or what it may look like. His heart was leading him for the first time in a long time and he wasn't about to ignore that she wasn't okay.

Moving in front of her, he waved his hands around himself, gesturing to his wheelchair and leg. "Sorry, but... this is personal. This whole shit is personal. You come in here and talk about my personal life and expect me to trust you, but you don't open up with what's going on in your life. Talk to me, or I don't talk to you." His threat hung heavy in the air.

Alex shifted to her left hip and gave him a look with her eyebrows. "This is my job. Getting you to talk and forget what is going on is what worked for you. I didn't do it to use against you or be mean, and it wasn't even super personal information that you gave. I'm paid to help you. But you aren't a therapist, okay?"

His eyes never left her face. The more he looked at her, the more he realized she was definitely not herself. When he met her, she didn't have a drop of makeup on. Her eyes shimmered. He'd thought about her smile all week. Today, she had heavy makeup on her left eye and they looked sad. A slight reddish-pink rimmed them as if she'd been crying. Someone had hurt her.

"Look, I don't believe in knights and shining armor. I don't need someone swooping in and saving me," she groused.

"Yeah, swooping is bad, we wouldn't want that." His droll tone shocked her. "Look, I don't believe in that shit either, I'm just a guy with a gun--er, I was anyways. That doesn't mean you can clam up. Talk to me, please? You have my back, I'll have yours. Clear?"

"Hrmp," she grunted in response.

"So, what's the malfunction, soldier?"

"How do you know I served?" Suspicion clouded her gaze faster than he could blink.

"Ha, that's easy. Your demeanor *screams* military. You can take the civilian out of the soldier, but you can't take the soldier out of the civilian. So, what branch?"

"Air Force, but that was just to pay for college. I enjoyed my time serving my country and ultimately that's why I'm a therapist specifically with the VA. I feel my best work should be given to those who have served their country."

"That's quite a tear jerker. Look, I've almost cried," he jested.

Alex giggled and playfully pushed Darren, "Smart ass."

"My ass isn't smart! It's always talking shit behind my back."

Alex closed her eyes and shook her head.

Smiling with victory, Darren prodded her, "So, you going to tell me what was cooking last week?"

She sighed and rubbed her forehead, "Let's get the ball throwing then."

"Oh, God, more puns?"

Alex giggled. "Maybe a little."

Darren stood from his chair and headed for the railing. Alex joined him, scooping a ball on the way.

"We've solidified you can throw me the ball and I'm sure someone here's been beating you up for me for the week so let's work on your range of motion next, shall we?"

"Whatever you say, boss," he harassed.

"Back to back, soldier," she directed. She waited for him to get comfortable with a strong stance, walked around him and touched back to back. He was only a few inches taller than her, making the exercise much easier. Turning to her right, she handed him the ball on his left. He then moved the ball in front of himself and handed it to her left on his right. "Great job. Slow and steady."

"So, what was so terrible that you had to miss our lovely rendezvous?" Darren asked lightly while concentrating on the action. He put a little more effort in the movement than he cared to, but he was there to change and get stronger and she was certainly putting him through changes.

"Well, I have an ex..."

"Who doesn't? Let me guess... doesn't get it that he's an ex?" He continued taking and giving her the ball, their momentum picking up a bit as he fell into a nice rhythm with her.

"Precisely." She shifted her weight a bit. "Let's make things more difficult. I can already feel you getting too cozy over there, slacker." She reached up when passing him the ball and when going to get it back from him reached low, then she passed it back to her left, making him change directions. "If nothing else, I'll keep ya guessin'"

"Oh great, just when I was getting comfortable, you make things hard again. Thanks."

"You're welcome," she answered.

"Surely you heard my sarcasm."

She nodded. "Still. You're welcome."

Chuckling, he said, "I like this. I feel a little tight in the waist and hips. I know it's because I was doing the same things for so long. This is brilliant." He cleared his throat nervously. "So, this forgetful fellow... Did he give you that shiner?"

She faltered for half a second before passing him the ball again. "You should see the other guy."

"Wouldn't be in his best interest for me to." The threat hung heavy in the air.

After a hefty silence, she said, "I just want him to stop bothering me. He's convinced we are good together and that I'm being irrational with how I feel, but I don't really think someone who throws things in anger is balanced enough to be my forever roommate."

Darren chuckled before he could stop himself. "Forever roommate?"

"My parents were amazing together, but didn't make it for the long haul. They've both remarried and their new spouses weren't the best and it just got to me. Though I would love to have the love my parents had, I just don't see it for myself, so I call the ultimate relationship forever roommates. If someone is willing to love me forever, they won't need a piece of paper to say I'm somehow their property. We will just fall in step with one another and be an amazing team that doesn't need conventional rules or whatever."

"While it sounds a little cynical, I can understand that. I've had a few relationships myself, but none I would call worthy either. I'm the job," he agreed.

"You said you were a sniper?" She took the ball and stepped away from him, stopping their exercise. Turning, she put her hand on his waist, sending a chill up his spine that settled warmly in his belly. Leading him to the chair, she put the ball down and sat by him. "Sorry. I know after that one, I get a little winded if we are going fast and then my equilibrium is a bit off. I wasn't implying—"

He cut her off. "I was a little shaky and appreciate the assist." Veering back on topic, he nodded, "Yes, I was a sniper."

"A lone wolf, you said?"

Another nod.

"Why? You're a strapping lad. You seem pretty decent, despite your awful jokes. Can't find someone to tolerate long? Or are you untrusting?" It wasn't an accusation, more of acknowledgment.

"I just have always worked better alone. I protect my brothers, my family, anyone I care for with all that I am, but in the end, I can't wait on someone else to do it. I have to," he answered honestly. "When that IED took us out, I was pissed. It was my first emotion to be upset that my brothers were there. I can scout alone."

"You mean die alone?" She walked to a supply cabinet, grabbed a few things, and came back.

"I'm more careful when it's just me. I listen more. I think for myself. I try not to feel secure in a group, but it's easy to get lazy in one, you know? I don't want others to get hurt," he rationalized.

"So, they are more valuable than you are?"

He shook his head. "It's not that."

"Well, what is it?" she asked as she cracked an ice pack. Removing his prosthesis, she applied the ice pack and wrapped a bandage around the edge to keep it secure before wheeling him to the window and sitting back down.

"I can't help how I think. It's always been just easier alone. Me and the target. I can shut everything else off, do my job, and go home," he shrugged. Saying it out loud to her sounded stupid, but even when he was a kid, group things were fun, but never as fun as working on a puzzle alone or doing some other activity where he was his only competition.

"I'm the same way, honestly. I was an only child growing up and have never had a lot of people around. When I do, I can handle it, but I certainly don't love it as much as I love a good book or movie in my own space. When I served, people thought I was weird because I would eat and go to my room instead of hang out with everyone. I knew it was great for morale and did it sometimes, but I need that quiet time to center myself." She sounded peaceful as she watched the sunset.

"Did anyone ever give you a nickname?" he asked out of the blue.

"I don't think I've ever been close enough to anyone," she said, sounding almost mystified that it had never occurred to her before. "Man, maybe I'm a hermit." She chuckled at herself.

"They used to call me Mist."

"Ooh," she sounded intrigued immediately. "Why? Because you're one with nature and blend into your surroundings like the morning dew? Or because your presence is light and lovely but can snuff out the weak?" Her conspiracy theories rallied for a few more moments.

"No, because if I ever didn't make my target, I could say that I missed... and no one would realize I was a bad shot."

She deadpanned. "Get out. It's time for you to go. No more jokes today, sir. That's enough out of you."

"What? It never happened. It was a safeguard I maneuvered in place just in case." She wheeled him to the door while a laugh tugged at her lips.

"You are terrible and becoming more and more like a pirate every day. Hey, Mist works for pirates as well. I'm sure there's a bad omen about mist and death out there somewhere," she added extra r sounds at the end of her word to punctuate it.

"You're just as bad as me," he laughed. "See you tomorrow?"

When she looked nervous, but nodded, he added, "Pirate promise?"

"What on earth is a pirate promise?"

Taking on a pirate-like voice, he said, "That be where if ye don't show up fer yer session, I make ye walk the plank." He shook his head at himself. "Okay, that was awful, but someone can definitely walk the plank if you need them to."

"No promises, but I will try my very best."

"That will do nicely," he said. "Goodnight, Alex."

"Night, Pete," she chided as she walked toward the employee lounge to get her things.

♥

"You certainly seem excited for your therapy session today."

"Do I?" Darren shrugged to his friend, Jones, as they drove toward the offices the next day. "I'm making great progress and-"

"Finally," Jones interjected. "You're *finally* making progress. I was sure you'd never give it a true whirl."

"And," Darren continued with force in his voice, poking back at his friend for being a brat. "It's hurting less when I use this thing," he tapped on the leg. "I'm feeling stronger, too. Maybe I might actually have a shot at a real life at some point."

"I'm glad. Whatever turned it all around for you, good! You're one of the coolest dudes I know, man. I'm sure you're going to outrun me in no time."

"That shouldn't be too difficult, when was the last time you ran?"

"Ouch, that almost hurt!" Jones feigned pain in his chest. "Dude, I pulled a hamstring. I'm on the injured reserve list."

"Two months ago," Darren deadpanned before chuckling. "Quit babying your leg and get out there. I don't even have half of mine and I'm out here getting it. Plus, you gotta keep your girlish figure going, right?" Grinning, he pulled himself out of the car and made his way toward the trunk to get his wheelchair.

"Hey, man, I gotta pay them bills somehow!" shouted Jones from the driver's seat as he pressed the interior button to pop the trunk. He glanced in his rearview mirror to check on his buddy, but didn't move from his seat, knowing all too well that Mr. Lone Wolf had to do things on his own the moment he could. In the last handful of weeks, he'd seen his friend improve greatly. He'd always set the curve on improvement, but recently he'd really stepped it up a notch and was far more mobile with or without assistance. He was impressed with his determination and dedication.

"Maybe your stripper name should be Glitter," Darren mused as he eased into his wheelchair and tapped the back of the car to let his friend know he was done.

Chuckling, Jones said, "It's on the very short list, don't worry. I'll see you in an hour, Mist. Try not to flirt too hard with the ladies in there."

"Don't you have somewhere to be rather than here harassing me?"

"You take the fun out of everything, you know."

As Jones drove off, Darren wheeled himself into the PT office. "Hello, Jessica. I'm here for my daily butt-kicking with Alex."

"I'm sorry, Darren. She's not in today, something came up. You'll be working with Tony today."

"She's not in? Is she ok?" His mind went to work as he thought of their convos.

"Yeah, she just said that something personal came up and had to take the day off and that she was really sorry."

"Ah, I see. Thank you. Do you mind if I cancel my appointment today? The last couple of sessions really worked my leg and it's pretty sore. I could use the day off, too, if I'm being honest with myself," he reached down and rubbed his leg for extra effect.

"Sure thing. I hope your leg feels better tomorrow, hun."

Darren smiled at the receptionist and nodded, "Thanks, me, too." Turning his phone on to call Jones to come back, he thought of Alex and of her personal issue. He couldn't do anything about it, but it bugged him nonetheless. She was such a beautiful person and this jerk was sucking the life out of her. Not only personally, but was keeping her from doing her job as well. He knew that probably bothered her even more because she was passionate about her work.

"Hey, Jones, I decided to take the day off and let my leg rest. Would you mind coming back to pick me up?"

"Sure, man. I didn't make it too far anyway. Mind if we swing by the market on the way back? I need to pick up a few things on my way home and was going to do it after."

"Sure, let's do this," Darren agreed as he rolled out of the office to appreciate the sun on his face for a few minutes before Jones returned.

♥

"You okay, brother?" Jones asked as he pulled up minutes later. "That woman kicking your butt too much? Or did you get scared she was gonna bite?"

Darren chuckled. "Nah, just thought I'd take the day off since she took the day off, too."

"Oh, so y'all both playing hooky? Must be wearing each other out." He punctuated his sentence with an eyebrow waggle that went ignored.

"Pretty much. So, what is this market we're going to?"

Jones carefully pulled away from the curb. "It's a new farmers market. Because this isn't my regular side of town, I don't usually get to go, but I have a craving tonight, so we're going. It's got a lot of fruits, vegetables and homemade baked goods there. Sometimes there's a couple of extra booths that sell candles, honey, and tea - all really earthy stuff. I go for the homemade baked goods myself. Nothing quite hits the spot like warm baked goods." Turning to look at his friend with a wide smile he chimed, "But we could get you some nice, fresh fruits and veggies for your salads or whatever it is you birds eat these days."

Darren chuckled, "Someone has to be the fit one. I've been really craving some cheesy pasta lately and I need to pick up some food anyway, so this works out."

Pulling into the farmers market was chaos. Cars were pulling in and out, people weren't using the parking lot lines properly, pedestrians were walking every which way.

"Man, this place is chaotic!"

Jones smiled and looked around trying to find a safe spot. "Yep, they just started this market not too long ago and it's become very popular. All by word of mouth even. I guess there's a lot of birds in this town."

"Am I going to be able to get my wheelchair through this mess?"

"Don't worry. It's always chaos at the entrance, but once you get past the parking lot, you'll be fine. Trust me," he added as he parked in a roomy spot close to the door.

Darren looked at his friend with a weary expression. "My life is in your hands."

"Bahaha, just drama! Come on, let's get going." Jones enthusiastically jumped out of the car and popped open the trunk for his friend.

"I hope they have peach cobbler today. I tried it the first time I came and am addicted now. Whoever makes that, I'd marry them!"

Darren's eyebrow shot up in question. "Even if they were 70 years old?"

"Don't judge me!"

As they made their way through the chaos, the two of them chatted, dodging toddlers and passerby that were more concerned with their phones than with what was in front of them.

"Welcome to the market, man. This side is the fruits, that side is the vegetables, and over there you'll find dried meats and various other things. Ooh, it looks like the tea tent is up. You like tea, right?" The excitement in Jones voice was like a kid at Christmas.

"I do, indeed. I'll go check it out in a bit. There's the baked goods. Let's check those out since it's closer. Plus, I'd like to meet your future wife," Darren chuckled.

Wheeling up to the stand there were breads, pies, cookies, cakes, and pastries of all kinds. "Oh my goodness, how does one not get fat in this place?"

The owner who was a short, chubby woman grunted at Darren and shouted. "Who says we aren't?" as she patted her rounded belly.

He chuckled and wheeled over to her, "Do you make all these?"

"Me and my sisters. We do all the baking at home," the owner said proudly.

"Well, I have a marriage proposal from my friend Jones over there to the one that makes the peach cobbler," he grinned.

Jones looked up swiftly and blushed as he started to stammer. "Well, uh, you know, the, um, cobbler, I, uh, it's good and uh, I was just paying respects to the baker! That's all!"

The owner laughed heartily, "Honey, you couldn't keep up with me or my cooking if you tried! I'd have you in an exhausted diabetic coma in two days."

Jones grinned, "Well it would be worth it!" winking at the owner.

"So, you like my peach cobbler, then?"

"I do, yes. It's my absolute favorite. I come here every week hoping to grab one."

"Well, I'll be sure to make you one and hold it back here for you then," she smiled proudly. "It's always nice to have a fan of my work."

"It's the highlight of my week, ma'am! I look forward to next week then! Until then I'll take this apple pie and these pecan tarts, which I'm sure aren't as sweet as you," Jones added.

"Okay," she huffed and rolled her eyes with a chuckle as she headed to the cash register. "Enough with the flattery, I might have to pinch your cheeks or something."

"Hey, Jones, I'm headed over to the teas. I'll catch you at the fruits after?"

"Sure thing, Mist." He placed his small mound of treats on the counter and got out his wallet.

Darren slowly wheeled himself over to the teas as he checked out the other booths. One had homemade pasta and he immediately decided to buy some. He hadn't had homemade pasta since they'd been sent to Italy for a goodwill mission and his cravings never seemed to go away. After quickly purchasing the pasta and getting the shopkeepers card, he finally made his way over to the tea section. They were split into various stands and regions, each having its own unique smells and textures. There were even brewing pots and other contraptions he hadn't seen in his travels.

"Excuse me, sir, how does this steeper work?" he asked a gracefully aging smiling fellow at one of the kiosks.

"Well you put the loose tea or tea bag in bottom here and then fill this cup with your water. If you're a tea drinker, you know not all tea needs boiling water to steep," he shook his head to loosen his thoughts. "But yeah, so you put your water of choice in, then you place the whole thing over your cup or mug and then press down on the contraption. The boiling water will slowly pour through the hole where the tea is and pour into your cup."

"Huh, that sounds pretty interesting."

"It's an individual cup of tea maker and the taste is amazing. I sell them pretty cheap, but if you buy three boxes of tea, I'll throw in the tea maker for half off."

"What the heck, get me the Egyptian Licorice tea along with these two I already picked out and I'll buy your tea maker then," Darren said. He used to be a coffee drinker until they visited a few countries where they made tea. He was able to test different teas from different countries and found the healing advantages of it and as he didn't love the caffeine junk anyway, it seemed to be a nice fit. Something about a nice, hot cup of tea always settled his mind.

The old man noticed Darren's marines pin smiled. "Semper Fi," he said proudly, pointing to his own pin.

Darren smiled and responded, "Semper Fi," and saluted the older soldier.

Taking his bag, he almost turned before hearing a familiar voice. "Just let me look at the tea. You know I love my teas and I'm running low," she said in a hushed tone.

Darren turned around and rolled no more than a couple of feet and he was face to face with Alex.

Even behind her large sunglasses, he could see her look of genuine surprise. Standing menacingly next to her was a brick house of a man looking like someone stole his last lollipop.

Time froze as Darren and Alex exchanged a moment between each other. No words spoken, just an acknowledgement of each other's presence.

"Hey, Alex, how unexpected," Darren filled his voice with kindness. She seemed distressed and on edge and needed this. "I just came from therapy and decided I needed some pasta and tea. I'm a party animal, as you can see."

"Hey, h-how are you doing?" Her hesitance made him sad for her. She couldn't even speak in front of the guy, why waste her time with him?

Before he could answer, the guy moved to stand in front of her almost protectively. Over his shoulder, with his eyes locked on Darren, he asked, "Hey, do you know this guy Alexis?"

"He's no one. Just another soldier from the VA." Alex winced, her words seemed forced and almost as if it pained her to say them.

"Yeah, man, what's up? I'm Darren." He held his hand out, but He-Man didn't shake it. Putting his hand back down, he shrugged. "I get physical therapy where Alex works for my peg-leg issues." He bent down and knocked on his prosthesis.

"Huh. Fine then. You going to look at your stupid teas or what? We need to go," his gravelly voice came out so gruff, it sounded like he was voicing over a cartoon.

Deciding to cover his amusement, Darren turned his chair back toward the kiosk. "You like tea, too? I call myself a tea snob personally. I can't get enough of them. I definitely blame the traveling on that. Check out this doohickey," Darren lifted up the tea maker to Alex. "It makes an individual cup of tea that's steeped just right. You can even see it being done inside. It looks pretty cool, too. I couldn't say no to a fellow Marine apparently." Darren shot a smile at the kiosk owner.

Alex picked it up and looked at it. "Oh, that's so cool! I should get one. I could use one of these at work. No one there drinks tea. Coffee plagues the system," she chuckled.

"Yeah, yeah, that's all cute and shit. Come on, you're wasting my time!" The talking action figure grunted.

Darren clenched his fists and ground his teeth, but he refused to say anything to the man knowing now wasn't the time and he couldn't save Alex from her situation unless she wanted to be saved. He mused at what could they possibly be late for at this hour. Did he need to work out for the twentieth time today or what? Maybe he had reservations to eat a plate of kittens? Surely he was just late to do his community service or work at the soup kitchen. That was definitely it. He totally looked like a fine, upstanding citizen who wanted nothing more than to race to midnight mass on a weekday before donating blood and then topping the night off with some litter cleanup at a local park.

Darren snarfed to himself. Why did Alex tolerate this broken-down GI Joe anyway? He wasn't former military, that much was clear to Darren at first glance. Though he realized some disgraced the uniform by not being great people during their service or when they take off their uniform, Darren felt, in his heart, that once you are a soldier, you always were. Protecting was in his blood, but clearly not in Steroid Ken's.

"Hey, Alex," Darren said as he turned toward the next kiosk. "The sun is setting. I guess that means it's almost rest time, eh?" He nodded and smiled. A single show of support was all he knew he could give her, but wanted her to have it.

Alex swiped a lock of hair from face and smiled at him, saying 'thank you' with her eyes. She looked up and out of the glass of the front door and nodded. "You're right. Just about that time," she said softly as she turned back to look at the teas.

"What the fuck was that?" Darren could hear the Muscle-Milk swiller huff, but he didn't stay to listen.

He'd done all he could do for the moment and left the ball in her court. When she was ready to be rid of the guy, she would be. A moment later he chuckled to himself, "Heh, 'the ball's in her court'. That medicine 'ball' is going to kill me one of these days."

"Whoa, where's the fire?" Jones asked when Darren almost ran him over a moment later.

"Oh, there you are. I've shopped my leg off," Darren said with a cheeky grin as he pointed to the various bags that littered his lap. "Where have you been? Did you guys get hitched while I was shopping?" he asked, gesturing toward the baker who was still watching Jones from across the room.

"Not yet, but she did try to give me her number," Jones said with a slight blush.

"You're the one that offered marriage, bro. Don't wimp out on me now! Marines never give up, never surrender, right? Semper Fi. You know what it means," Darren added with a wink.

"Yeah, yeah, Hoo-rah. Let me get you out of here before I end up with a whole new family. I haven't even had dinner yet," Jones said as he rounded the back of the chair to start pushing.

"She would happily make you dinner. Stop playing around. You're turning your back on love," Darren teased. "Aww, it's okay. She's going to save you some hot cobbler for next week. Can I join you? We can go to Jared on the way here."

Apparently, engagement ring jokes were the final straw. "Don't make me leave you here with Stone Cold Steve Austin and the fox back there." When Darren chuckled and stayed silent, Jones went on, "Yeah, I saw that. He could have Whac-a-Mole'd you."

Darren shrugged. "I didn't say anything wrong. Ooh, stop here, I need some fresh cheese to go with this pasta. You wanna come over for dinner?"

Jones chuckled. "For your food? Heck yeah. You owe me for this harrassment."

"And look," Darren pointed to the bag hanging off of his friend's wrist. "You already have dessert."

Jones shot him a warning glance and Darren shut up. The guys had spent years of training together and were blessed to end up in the same town years later. Having a brother nearby when you had no other family always made a place feel like home.

♥

After the impromptu three-day weekend off from therapy, Darren was warming up for his session when Alex strolled in from the employee lounge. A beautiful smile lazily stretched itself across her face when she saw him. "Pete! How goes your sea adventures?"

"They be slowly progressin', ma'am. Gotta chip a few barnacles off me hull and I'm good to go," Darren teased. "If I'm a pirate, does that make you a saucy wench? You still need a nickname, in my humble opinion."

She chuckled. "I'd really rather not be a wench. I'm sure you can come up with something better."

"I'll put it on my to do list then," he said with a nod. "How do you plan to beat me up today?"

"Actually, I'd like to take a walk with you."

Startled, he almost stumbled over his words to try to do something else, but before he could fight it, she added, "I'm not taking no for an answer. It doesn't have to be far. I know you can do it."

Realizing he wasn't going to win, he shakily stood up. "Where to?"

She motioned her head toward the large window, she stole a glance at the clock. "We have about fifty minutes to make it that far. Think you can handle it?"

"Soft floors and the prettiest drill sergeant I ever saw? Sure, I can do this."

Standing beside him, but not touching, Alex lowered her voice. "Thank you."

"Well, I'm just doing what you told me to, so thank you," Darren answered in true guy fashion.

"No, I mean for the other night at the market," she seemed embarrassed and hid behind her hair for a moment. "I could tell you didn't want to be so calm, but you did, and it meant so much to me. Thank you."

"You don't seem to be the type that needs saving and I just thought you could use a reminder of your worth," he managed as he cautiously took another step forward. He hadn't walked more than three feet without rails in months. It was taking almost all of his focus to stay upright, his eyes were locked onto his feet and the carpet ahead of him.

Lowering her voice even more, she added, "I kicked him out and filed a restraining order on him."

Darren stopped and looked up at her. "What? Are you okay? Did he hurt you?" He glanced over her to check for signs of injury.

Chuckling, she guided. "Get back to what you're doing." He quickly complied. "I'm great, actually. He didn't get a chance to hurt me. Something in what you said reminded me that I'm strong, but deserve my rest. Every night he has these adventures planned to prove to me how strong and awesome he is. He was actually exhausting. If I didn't want to go do something, he accused me of things. If someone looked at me, he'd accuse me of sleeping with them or any other ridiculous thing and, well, I was already fed up with him, I just didn't do anything about it. I don't know why I didn't. I guess maybe I thought I'd be lonely or that I was being dumb for wanting him to be nicer to me." She sighed. "Saying that out loud just sounds lame."

"Well, you deserve way better than that. A real man who will support and love you," Darren started before almost tripping. He righted himself before continuing. "One that will push you to great things and rest with you when it's time. Life isn't about going until you can't go anymore. Of course, everyone has goals and wants to reach them, but you have to enjoy the down time, too. It took this to open my eyes to that," he said, gesturing toward his leg.

She nodded and wrapped her hand around his arm.

"I'm okay," he said.

"Yeah, I know," she squeezed and released him. "I... I just wanted to show my appreciation and am not really supposed to fraternize..."

"Oh." Embarrassed, he realized she had just flirted with him and he's basically shunned her while being proud of himself. It had never occurred to him that she would be interested in *him*. He wasn't even able to actually walk. She was a beautiful, vibrant woman who needed someone good, but he didn't suspect he was in the running for such a position. He chuckled to himself when he thought about running.

"I'm... I'm sorry. I didn't expect..." she stumbled over her words and tried to step away from him.

Reaching out, he grabbed her hand. He looked toward the desk and saw no one was around. "Relax and walk with me? I already made it this far," he pointed out, gesturing toward the window that was only about ten feet away now. "I should make it by the time our favorite view is ready for us."

She seemed to be almost disappointed but continued walking alongside Darren, no longer speaking.

They reached the window just in time to see the sunset in all of its glory. Darren sat as quickly as possible on one of the stacks of exercise mats, Alex stood a few feet away, staring out the window, a sadness seemed to hide in her eyes.

"Care to take a load off?" Darren offered as he patted the mats next himself. There was plenty of room for both of them to sit.

"I should go get your chair," she muttered and turned to talk away.

Lowering his voice to where he knew only the two of them could hear it, he asked, "Please?" He reached out and lightly touched her hand, freezing her in place. His fingers intertwined with hers at an awkward angle as he tugged her closer.

She sat, releasing his hand as she locked her eyes on the sunset again. "I didn't mean to—"

"Please let me correct an error before you continue," Darren requested. "I was hyper focused on walking just now and completely didn't see what was happening. I wasn't ignoring you and that chuckle was definitely not about you. It was more me laughing at my inner demons for chastising me constantly."

She stayed silent, but her lip quivered slightly.

Leaning forward, his hand brushing against hers before he took it and placed a kiss on her hand. "What I should have asked ages ago was, Alexis, would you care to join me for dinner?"

Her eyes softened, and a small smile danced on her lips. "We aren't supposed to fraternize—"

"You're fired!" he interjected with a chuckle. "I'm not asking you for more than a meal right now, I'm just asking if a hard-working, strong, beautiful woman would like a nice meal with a very grateful man who wants nothing more than to spoil her with his amazing cooking skills. Even if it's just one night I get to spend with you, that would be a true gift to me. It doesn't need to be called a date or anything like that if you don't want it to be."

Stealing a glance toward where her co-workers would normally be watching everything, she noticed no one was around and she nodded. "Okay, but I should cook."

"Why? Think I can't handle myself?" he teased. "I'll have you know I spent time in Italy and am an honorary Italian when it comes to cooking. Ask Mama Rosita in Santa Marinello. She taught me everything she could in the three weeks I was there. I can make you a pasta primavera that will make you weak in the knees."

She smiled at his enthusiasm. "No, I just feel like I owe you or something from yesterday."

He could see she felt unsure still because of his perceived spurning of her advanced. "I owe you for helping me find my footing," he chuckled at his unintentional pun. "Honestly. It would be my honor and pleasure if you'd join me. Any man would be an absolute fool not to want to spend time with you."

Another blush rose to her cheeks. "Deal. Let me know when," she said as she started to stand again, as he finally released her hand from when he kissed it.

"Tonight too soon?" he chuckled. "I'm eager, what can I say?"

She joined him with a giggle. "Fair enough. I've actually daydreamed about hanging out with you many times, so... I'm excited."

It was his turn to blush.

"But first, stay for another minute or two, please? This is the best part," he gestured toward the sunset. They watched the sun dip behind the horizon and silently sat together for a few more moments before Alex went to get Darren's chair.

"Any ideas on the time I should be at your place?" she asked softly as she pushed Darren to the front of the office.

"I could cancel my ride and we could go right now," he teased.

"Great, just let me get my coat," she said as she turned to get her things from the lounge. "By the way, it's totally a date."

He chuckled. "As you wish, ma'am."

Shut Up and Kiss Me
Lissa Lynn Thomas

Friday night in a small town is a dependable sort of creature. The adults who are so inclined congregate at the saloon, while those who've left high school but haven't reached the legal drinking age yet find their own fun in town park, weather permitting. Unless you'd rather keep your fun private. There are plenty of out-of-the-way spots sprinkled through our little town where people can hide away from the rest of the populace if desired. That's usually where I can be found, away from the eyes of the townsfolk who see everything and talk too much.

Jo, my girlfriend since our sophomore year in high school, is in the passenger seat of my beat-up truck, glaring out her window. Apparently, she'd rather stare into nothing than look at me and continue the argument we've been having. Lately, this is what our Friday nights together have looked like. One or both of us upset, trying to make our point of view understood by the other. Neither of us ever really gain any ground. With our college graduation coming up, we knew this was coming, but I don't think either of us expected it to be this hard. Or maybe that was just me. Maybe this is why she kept trying to break things off, saying it would be for the best if she let me go.

I study her profile as she avoids my gaze, the lush mouth turned down at the corners, the hollows in her cheeks, the tear tracks under her eyes. I swallow hard, the expanse of seat between us suddenly feels vast, unsurmountable, and I reach out to try and take her hand, but she stiffens. Her arms come around herself, as though to protect herself from what I might say next.

Okay, give her space, I think.

I drop my hand back to my lap, feeling defeated. "Please, Jo, talk to me. You know I can't take it when you shut me out like this."

"I don't know what you want me to say, Cash." She sounds tired and sad, and I hate myself for causing it, but I can't deny who I am or what I want to do with my life. Not for anyone. "We've talked about it, I've told you how I feel," she says, her shoulders coming up defensively. "You're going anyway."

I feel her words like a physical blow. I hate that I'm hurting her, hate that she can't see any positive outcomes for us if I go after what I want. I try and tamp down the growing hurt that she can't be supportive of my goals, like I am of hers. "You're looking at this like if I go, I'm never coming back. It's not a lifelong prison sentence, Jojo, it's a tour of duty. I get to do what I've always wanted—serve my country. Like my dad did."

My dream since I was a boy has been to join the army and serve my country, to help protect our nation. I had originally planned to go after my high school graduation, but Mom had different plans. She made me promise to go to college first, and then, she said, I was free to do what I like. She understands my need to do this, even if she doesn't like it. She wanted to make sure I'd still have a future if I decided the army wasn't for me after all, once my time had been served. Her words, not mine.

"Your dad *died*, Cash. Are you forgetting that part? Your mom was left to raise you on her own. She was left all alone." Her voice breaks on the last words. "I don't understand why you want to leave me," she practically whispers.

The hell with trying to give her space, I think, and scoot closer to her, gathering her in my arms, ignoring the tension in her posture. "Jo, you know better than that," I say, hoping I'm right. "I don't ever want to leave you, and I promise you that I'll come back for you. Nothing's gonna keep me from being with you forever. I told you that." I try to inject every ounce of my determination into the statement, to prove to her I mean it and I truly believe it. Our story isn't done. We have a whole lifetime to live together.

But can't I do that and follow my dream? Does it have to be one or the other?

She raises sad hazel eyes to mine and I watch a new tear trickle down her face. I wipe it away with the pad of my thumb, lean down and kiss her cheek, hold her closer.

"I'm scared," she whispers into my shirt and I feel the tension leave my shoulders. At least she's sharing it now. I rub her back, keeping her against me.

"So am I. I'm so scared of losing you," I admit without shame.

She huffs a sigh at me, "If that was the case, you wouldn't still be going on about this." Her words lack venom, she simply sounds resigned. She's still expecting the worst. She's just made the decision in her head to stop talking about it. I swallow a sigh of my own and kiss the top of her head.

"I love you," I tell her almost desperately, trying to bring her out of the darkness that seems to constantly be on the verge of swallowing her whole. "It's going to be okay."

"Just shut up and kiss me, Cash," she begs, tilting her head up to mine, so our lips graze softly. "Please?" I shudder a little.

'Shut up and kiss me' is sort of a running joke between us. It started the night of our first date when I walked her to her door and stood there babbling at her like an idiot. I was debating whether or not I should risk a kiss when she stepped closer to me, rested her hands on my shoulders and tilted her face up to mine and said softly, "Cash?"

I immediately ceased my stammering at her proximity and gulped. "Y-yeah?"

Her big hazel eyes danced up at mine. "Shut up and kiss me," she said with a saucy grin. And so, I did.

And I do the same now. I kiss her like I'll never get the chance again, like she's the air I need to breathe. I kiss her until we're both breathing heavily, fogging the windows of the truck. I kiss her until there's no doubt, no fear. Only us.

♥

Two hours later, I walk in my front door and toss the keys to my truck in the bowl Mom keeps on the table in the entryway. I toe off my sneakers so as not to track dirt through the house and incur her wrath. It's almost midnight, she's most likely in bed already. She works harder than anyone I've ever known. She's a nurse in the emergency room at the local hospital. I try to be as respectful of her sleep time as I can be. With that in mind, I do my best to be quiet as I head for the kitchen and a glass of water before turning in myself. I'm surprised to find Mom sitting up in her robe at the kitchen table, a steaming mug in front of her. Her long blonde hair is in a single braid that falls down her back. She smiles at me, but she looks drawn, her brown eyes tired.

I stoop and drop a kiss on the top of her head, and she reaches up and pats my cheek affectionately. "What are you doing up? Everything okay?" I ask as I go to the tap and draw myself a glass of water.

She yawns and nods, "I'm fine, son. Just a long night. We lost a kid tonight, car accident." I frown and come back to the table with my water. "It never really gets easier."

I reach across the table and take her hand, give it a squeeze. "I'm sorry, Mom. I'm sure you did all you could for them, though."

She blinks tears out of her eyes and nods at me, looking embarrassed at being caught so vulnerable. Normally, she wields what I call her game face like a shield to keep her sadness from showing.

"You're out late," she says, clearly trying to deflect and I nod, allowing it.

"Just dropped Jo off at home." I sigh, remembering that we still haven't really resolved our issue. Mom rests her chin on her hand, propping her elbow on the table and tilts her head to watch my face.

"You two okay?" she asks, and I nod, downing the rest of my water, making to get up and retreat to my bedroom. She tightens her hold on my hand as I move to stand and says, "Oh, no you don't. Sit back down." Her tone brooks no resistance and I slump back in my chair. She meets my eyes and says simply, "Talk."

I look at the table as I sigh again. "She's still not okay with me enlisting." Mom makes a soft noise of what, I'm not sure, but I'm sure it doesn't bode well for me. "And I can't make her see things my way."

Mom squeezes my hand, "Cash, sweetheart, I love you, you know that, and I adore Johanna. Really, I do," she insists at my dubious glance. "But you're never going to get her to see things your way, monkey. She doesn't. But she does love you." Mom sounds pensive when she adds, "I sometimes worry she loves you too much and herself not enough."

I swallow hard, feeling that statement in the pit of my stomach. It's true. Jo wrestles with depression and doesn't see all the amazing things others see in her. I tell her as often as I can, but most of the time, she doesn't seem to hear me. It doesn't matter how brilliant and funny I think she is. It doesn't matter that I love her more than I thought possible. I don't know who I would be without her. I look at Mom and bite my lip, considering. "Any sage advice you'd care to bestow on me?"

She holds my eyes a moment and lets out a breath. "As much as I'd love for you to do *anything* else with your life, you've wanted to follow in your daddy's footsteps since you were a little boy. I know you love Jo, and I know she loves you. But sometimes, love's not enough, monkey." She smiles sadly at me, trying to take the sting out of her words, but I asked so she's going to give it to me straight. "You have to be fair to both of you, and ask yourself are you *both* going to be happy in five years? Ten?"

Mom's right, but I feel the bottom of the world fall out from underneath me thinking of ending my relationship with Jo. My chest hollows out, my stomach flipping with grief at the imagined loss. How could I ever let her go when I love her so much?

But how can I keep her tethered to me when she's so afraid of the life I want for myself? How is that fair to her?

I look at Mom and she stands up from her seat and comes around the table to hug me. "I'm sorry, I know that's not what you wanted to hear," she tells me softly. She kisses my cheek. "Just be certain before you make any important decisions, Cash."

♥

College graduation approaches and my thoughts chase themselves around my head in circles as I try to find the perfect solution to the issue at hand. That is, the solution that doesn't include letting go of the woman I love. Mom said I should be sure before I make any decisions. But I only know this: I love Johanna with all of my heart and I always will. I also want to serve my country more than I've ever wanted to do anything else. I don't want to choose between them. I want her forever *and* I want to be a soldier.

Inspiration hits one night when I'm rifling through my nightstand, searching for spare batteries for the TV remote. Instead, I find a little velvet box. Batteries forgotten now, I take out the box and flip the top open, revealing a princess cut platinum engagement ring. I've had this plan in the works for a while now. I was waiting for the night of our joint graduation party. Here is something that I've never doubted, something I had decided a long time ago--like the night of our first date. I saved up for years to be able to afford the perfect ring for her, finally purchasing it three months ago. Being with Jo forever has felt inevitable since that first night, that first kiss sealed my fate. I'll never love anyone else. This should prove that to her. It has to, the alternative is too horrible to consider further.

♥

Graduation day is finally here. I'm a ball of nervous energy, my very blood trembling with anticipation and anxiety. Mom seems to know something's up even though I haven't told a soul about my plan to propose. It's a super power of hers, knowing when I'm plotting something. It was quite upsetting when I was younger, I could never get away with anything. Before the party, I run around trying to reassure myself that I have everything I'll need. At the florist shop I pick up my order of a dozen pink roses, Jo's favorite. A giant red heart-shaped helium balloon is already waiting in my truck. Normally, this is something I would do privately, I'm not one for big scenes. Jo needs reassurances, though, so this will be a little bit of a spectacle. She's worth it.

    I think between Mom and Jo, the entire town has been invited to this shindig tonight. Mom's bought enough food and drinks for a small army. I attempt to douse my nerves as I help Mom set up the back yard. Jo went inside to get dressed. I opted for casual, knowing I'm already going to be a nervous wreck, I don't need to be dressed up like someone else and make it worse. I have simple khaki cargo shorts on with a white tank under an open blue short sleeved button-down shirt. Jo reemerges in a pretty pink sundress that falls right to her lovely tanned knees and matching sandals. Her long dark hair is pulled back in a high ponytail, her face free of makeup. She's never looked more gorgeous in my eyes.

    I wait until the party is in full swing, and signal to Raif Montgomery, the lead singer of Renegades, the band comprised of our old high school friends that Mom hired to play the party, that it's time. Raif grins at me and nods. He's my only conspirator since the guys arrived and I dragged him aside to let him know what I needed from him. He leans into the microphone and says, his voice smooth and low, "Okay, folks, let's all quiet down for a moment. Cash has something he'd like to say."

    The crowd quiets slowly, and I feel all the eyes in the backyard turn to me and I smile at Jo, leaning in and kissing her softly on the mouth before holding up one finger. "One sec, sorry everyone," I say, my hands shaking now that the time has come. I dash to my truck and return with the roses and balloon and find Jo still standing where I left her, her normally pale cheeks flushed and her eyes wide. Mom is sitting at a table a few feet away from us, her face blank as she watches the scene unfold.

Jo's lips tremble as she takes the bouquet I offer her. "Cash," she murmurs, "what's going on?" She sounds terrified and I smile at her, hoping I don't look as scared as I feel inside.

"Those are for you, Jojo. And so is this," I say, handing over the balloon. She grins at me despite her nerves and tilts her head to the side, regarding me as though I'm an animal that might suddenly bite her.

"Thank you," she says softly, hugging the roses to her chest, her grip tight on the balloon string as she looks at me. I hear Luke's fiddle start playing low, Shania Twain's *From This Moment On*, as I requested. Her eyes get wider as she recognizes her favorite song.

I clear my throat and take her hand with the balloon string in it, dropping down to one knee in front of her. I hear the collective murmurs and gasps from our family and friends, here to celebrate with us. My eyes stay on the face of the woman of my dreams, my insides squirming unpleasantly with nerves. She looks shocked, but not unhappy. I reach into my jeans pocket and pull out the ring box, but don't open it yet. I smile at her as her pretty pink mouth falls open.

"You cast your spell on me a long time ago, Jo," I tell her honestly. "Neither of us is perfect, but I believe we're perfect for each other. I don't ever want to be without you. I know things won't always be easy, but I promise you that I'll *never* give up on us. You *own* my heart. I love you so much, Jo." I blink the moisture from my eyes, flip open the ring box, holding it up so she can see it clearly and ask, "Johanna Lynne Bridges, would you do me the honor of becoming my wife?"

Her eyes flood with tears as she sinks down onto her knees in front of me, squishing her roses between us as she hurls herself into my arms, holding me like I'll disappear if she lets me go. I wrap her in my embrace, my hand on the back of her head, cradling her skull, still waiting for her answer. She's shaking—or I am? I can't tell anymore. I duck my head to find her eyes, and she smiles at me so huge that it takes my breath away. "Yes," she whispers, "yes, I'll marry you."

I let out a whoop of pure joy and she laughs, and we kiss to raucous applause and shouts. I hold Jo tight to my chest and whisper to her, "Thank you."

She grins at me, her face alight, her eyes dancing with mischief as she whispers back, "Shut up and kiss me, Cash."

♥

Three weeks later, I heft my new bride into my arms and carry her across the threshold of the house we've rented. We finished moving in before the pre-dawn hours this morning. Jo giggles, her arms looped loosely around my neck as I try and maneuver her through the narrow doorway without braining her, and I smile wide at the pure joy of the sound. I need more of her laughter in my life. I lean in and kiss her with everything I feel for her. I kiss her until her hands move from around my neck to my face, touching my jaw. When I break away to breathe, I rest my forehead against hers and simply enjoy her nearness.

"I love you, Mrs. Vereen," I tell her with the huge smile I haven't been able to wipe off my face since the judge pronounced us man and wife a few hours ago. I watch a matching smile break over her beautiful face and I kiss her once more and then finally step into our new home, using my foot to close the front door behind us.

"Put me down, put me down," Jo pleads, kicking her feet as I continue holding her in my arms. I dip her back as if I might drop her and she squeals and tightens her hold on me. I chuckle, raising her back up and kissing her again, laughing into her mouth.

"Welcome home," I say, setting her down on her feet again. I don't remove my hands from her hips until I'm sure she's steady. Jo immediately comes back into my space and wraps her arms around my middle, resting her head on my chest. I hold her to me and breathe her in. She smells of sunshine and fluffy clouds, of grass and daisies. It's how she always smells, like a sunny spring day. I do my best to commit the combination to my memory to reflect on when I leave next month.

Jo still isn't exactly excited about it, but she says we'll make it work. She's trying so hard to be positive and I'm so proud of her, but there is also a nagging sense of guilt eating away at me inside. I know it'll be hard for her when I'm gone, but I was too selfish to let her go. I don't like what that says about me, but I push the thought away. Today is a happy day. Our mothers went with us to city hall and witnessed for us, then surprised us with a cookout afterwards. It was a perfect day, full of friends and laughter and toasts to our happiness. Jo's smile has been incandescent all day, her eyes shining with excitement and I'm trying to record every moment to my memory, to hold on to that look on her face, the way she looks in her yellow slip dress.

We stand there like that, slightly swaying and hanging onto each other, lost in our own heads for I don't know how long before Jo looks up at me, her hazel eyes alight. "I think I need a guide to find our bedroom," she says, her voice low and husky. She grins, coming up on her toes to kiss me and I fall into it, letting myself get caught up in the sensations. My hand comes up into the silky length of her mahogany hair, which is hanging unadorned to the middle of her back. I run my fingers through it while our mouths meet hungrily, our bodies pressed tightly together now. Our tongues tangle and dance and Jo's hand sneaks under the bottom of my button-down shirt so I feel her warm fingers on the bare skin of my stomach.

I groan into her mouth as lust short circuits my brain, my hand tightening in her hair. I break the kiss for a moment, trying to regain reason so our wedding night isn't memorable for all the wrong reasons. She presses closer to me and I move my hands to her hips, lifting her easily. I breathe slowly, working to slow the pounding of my blood in my veins. She wraps her legs around my waist as our mouths meet again, *reason be damned*. I want her too badly to go slow tonight. I move my hands to her bottom and force my mouth from hers, force my eyes open so I can walk without banging us both off the walls. Her mouth finds its way to my neck where she kisses and nips at my skin, making the fire burn hotter inside me. I turn and make my way through the living room and down the short hallway until I'm at the second door on the left. Our bedroom.

I stride inside and with her still in my arms, I kneel on our bed, let Jo's back hit the mattress and press my body against hers without letting her go. She sighs with pleasure, her legs still hooked around me, her dress bunched up around her thighs and I force myself to pause and take her in before I pounce on her. I sit back, move my hands slowly from her behind to the smooth length of her exposed thigh, and up. Her cheeks are flushed, her hair a dark mass across the pillows, her eyes are closed, her lips parted as though waiting for my kiss. I take another mental picture, wanting to remember her like this. I let my fingertips skitter over her body; glancing lightly over her thigh, her center, across her belly and up her ribs, over her chest. I use both hands, watching her face as I cup her breasts over her dress, testing their weight in my hands, thumbs stroking her nipples into tight buds. A needy sound escapes her throat and her eyes flutter open again.

I lean down over her, claiming her mouth with my own, my hands moving to the zipper on the back of her dress. I feel her fingers working at the buttons on my shirt and then she's touching my bare skin again. I break our kiss to peel her dress off of her and then she has my shirt on the floor, my shorts undone, then they and my briefs are pooled around my knees as she explores my body with her deft hands. Our mouths fit together again, kissing feverishly. She pushes at me until I move onto my back for her and then I'm naked and so is she. She's glorious; all soft, hot curves. She's absolutely, heart-stoppingly beautiful. I know I'll never forget the privilege of seeing her this way. I'll never forget this night. Never.

♥

Six weeks later, Jo and I are standing together in the airport. She insisted on coming with me, seeing me off and while I'm glad she's here, I am dreading our goodbye and what it might do to her. We stopped off at Mom's and I kissed her goodbye there, I knew she wouldn't come to the airport. Mom made me promise I'll do my best to stay in touch with them both and promised me she and Jo would look after each other. That eased my mind a little, I know Mom will follow through on that promise. Jo will have the support and love of her own mother and mine, our friends will help her, too. *She will be okay*, I tell myself.

"What are you worrying about?" she asks me, watching my face. I flush, and meet her hazel eyes. I forget how well she knows me sometimes. She's dressed in a flowing paisley printed skirt in shades of pink and purple and a tank top, her hair braided away from her face. As I study her closer, though, I notice she looks a little pale. I pull her into my arms, breathing in her scent, trying to sear it into my brain.

What am I worried about? I muse silently. I'm excited about this step, for myself, but I'm terrified that I made a colossal mistake out of pure selfishness. I want Jo to be happy, too, and looking at her face right now, forcing myself to see the worry in her eyes, the sadness lurking there, waiting to overwhelm her the moment I walk away from her. She's not happy, she's miserable. Because of me. My heart plummets into my feet. I know she was happy to get married, happy to tie her life to mine, but this parting is not okay with her. But she's going to try and pretend it is for my sake. I should have listened to Mom; she was right and I'm a selfish bastard.

"Nothing," I lie, kissing the top of her head.

I'll make this up to her, I think to myself, pleading with myself for absolution and finding none. I'm ashamed of myself, this is not the man I wanted to be, the husband I wanted to be.

"Liar," she comments without heat. "I love you, Cash." Her voice is strained, and I meet her eyes again, lean down and kiss her hard and thorough, imprinting her taste and feel in my mind. Trying to comfort us both, trying to slow down time so I don't have to leave her like this.

"I love you, too, Jo. I love you so much." I run my hands over her back, memorizing the feel of her in my arms. I rest my cheek against the top of her head, unable to look in her eyes, knowing she'll see the shame in mine. "I'm gonna miss you so much, Jo," I whisper, my voice hoarse, tears threatening now that the time for goodbye has come.

"I have to tell you something, and I don't have any idea how you're going to feel about it." Her voice cracks and I go still, scared of what truths she's going to share. She pulls back to look into my face and I cup her face in my hands, her hands coming up to circle my wrists.

"What is it? You know you can tell me anything, Jo," I say, trying to control my own emotions.

"Um, well. . ." she tugs her bottom lip between her teeth, her jaw set and her eyes closing tight. I watch her swallow hard, a small sob escaping her, and I pull her against me again, cradling her head to my chest.

"It's okay, whatever it is. Take a breath," I say, endeavoring to sound calm and comforting despite the fact that my pulse is now thumping away like a drum.

She trembles in my arms for a few moments, working to get herself under control. When she speaks, it's so shocking, you could literally knock me over with a slight breeze. "I'm pregnant, Cash."

There's joy in her voice, along with the panic. And that eases the tight lump of fear in my chest. I feel a huge smile spread over my face. *A baby.* I'm gonna be a dad. I wouldn't want for her to be pregnant while she's on her own, but this is still good news. I'm silent, though, shock blanking out my language skills for the moment.

"I wasn't trying or anything, I would have told you—we would have talked about it beforehand. Oh, I hope you know that. I swear, it's just one of those things that happens sometimes, my doctor said—" she babbles, mistaking my silence for judgment or horror. She sounds like she might start sobbing in earnest at any second.

I pull back, showing her the giant smile on my face, press my pointer finger to her lips and whisper, "Jo."

I watch as her eyes fill with tears. "Yeah?" she murmurs timidly.

I grin bigger, and demand, "Shut up and kiss me."

This Soldier's Heart

About the Authors

This Soldier's Heart

Becky Elizabeth
Be Mine, Valentine
♥

Becky is currently 24 and from a little town in England just outside Liverpool - home to The Beatles! She has a boyfriend who often has to compete for her attention with a little ginger kitten called Rocket Raccoon, but she loves both of her boys more than anything else in the world! Becky has always been passionate about reading and has been writing since the age of just 4, when she still vividly remembers reading a short story aloud at school. Though her confidence for public speaking may have dwindled, her passion for writing has only grown. From poetry, to full length novels, words are a way to escape from the chaos of life, or even make sense of it. Becky doesn't dream of fortune and fame - she just hopes to live her dream of making a living from her dreams and hopes that maybe one day, her words might help someone just like her.

You can find Becky all over social media, where you can keep up to date with all the latest updates and find out more about the name behind the words.

Amazon— https://www.amazon.com/Becky-Elizabeth/e/B076QTBZZM
Facebook (novel)— https://www.facebook.com/BeckyElizabethAuthor/
Facebook (poetry)— https://www.facebook.com/BeckyElizabethPoet/

Allana Kephart
Beautiful Trauma
♥

Allana Kephart has been making things up and bending people to her will from a very young age. She loves animals, tattoos, music, laughing, and reading and you can usually catch her entertaining one of these things at any given time. She spends an obscene amount of time finding pretty new words and thinking up awful ways to torment her characters. When not writing, she can be found walking one of her many fur babies, working at a local pet supply store, or jamming out in her car. She lives in the beautiful state of Colorado with her fish and fur-babies.

Facebook— http://www.facebook.com/allanakephartwrites/
Twitter— @AllanaKephart
Goodreads— http://www.goodreads.com/author/show/7376577.Allana_Kephart
Amazon— https://www.amazon.com/Allana-Kephart/e/B00JOVDOF4

This Soldier's Heart

Sam Destiny
A Tagged Valentine

♥

Once upon a time there was a young girl with her head full of dreams and her heart full of stories. Her parents, though not a unit, always supported her and told her more stories, encouraging her to become what she wanted to be. The problem was, young Sam didn't know what she wanted to be, so after getting her A-levels she started studying Computer Science and Media. After not even one year she realized it wasn't what her heart wanted, and so she stopped, staying home and trying to find her purpose in life. Through some detours she landed an internship and eventually an apprenticeship in a company that sells cell phones. Not a dreamy career, but hey. Today she's doing an accounting job from nine-to-five, which mainly consists of daydreaming and scribbling notes wherever she can.

All through that time little Sam never once lost the stories in her heart, writing a few little of them here and there, writing for and with her best friend, who always told her to take that last step.

Only when a certain twin-couple entered her mind, bothering her with ideas and talking to her nonstop did she start to write down their story - getting as far as thinking she could finish it. Through the help of some author friends, and the encouragement of earlier mentioned best friend, little Sam, now not so little anymore and in her twenty-seventh year, decided to try her luck as an Indie author. She finished the story of the first twin, Jaden, and realized she couldn't ever stop. So, it really is only after five that the real Sam comes out. The one that hungers for love, romance, some blood, a good story, and, at the end of the day, a nice hot cup of Chai Tea Latte.

And if the boys are still talking to her, she'll write happily ever after.

Amazon— https://www.amazon.com/author/samdestiny
Website— https://www.samdestiny.com/
Facebook— https://www.facebook.com/SamDestinyAuthor
Twitter— https://twitter.com/SamDestinyAuthr
Street Team— https://www.facebook.com/groups/DestinysMorningstars/
Goodreads— https://goo.gl/pHfPJp
BookBub— https://www.bookbub.com/authors/sam-destiny

Bella Sterling
This Soldier's Heart

Bella Sterling is a hopeless romantic and lover of the written word. When she's not writing, she enjoys watching sappy movies and tv shows guaranteed to make her cry while snacking on chocolate. She's still waiting for her prince charming to arrive and carry her off to the castle where she's meant to live out her happily ever after.

Facebook—https://www.facebook.com/Bella-Sterling-795822887289359/

This Soldier's Heart

C.M. Lehsten
A Soldier's Enchantment

♥

    C.M. Lehsten has had a pen in one hand and pencil in the other for over 30 years writing poetry, short stories and continuing to work on her epic tales. She grew up in Western New York and has a wide range of hobbies and interests that range all the way from the supernatural to the natural. She is a romantic at heart, having been happily married to her best friend for decades. She is a proud mom and grandma!

Facebook— https://www.facebook.com/CMLehsten.Author/

This Soldier's Heart

Jamie Summer
Never Knew Goodbye
♥

  Jamie Summer is a native of Germany, where she lives with her husband and son. She's currently working on her next book and wishes there were 48 hours to the day so she could do everything she sets her sights on.
  Besides writing Jamie enjoys watching her son grow up, reading and watching way too many TV shows.

Facebook— www.facebook.com/authorjamiesummer
Twitter— @authjamiesummer
Instagram— www.instagram.com/AuthorJamieSummer
Website— www.authorjamiesummer.com

This Soldier's Heart

Arielle Adams
Restless
♥

Arielle Adams is a possible side effect of your medication...

Arielle Adams is a pen name for Allana Kephart's poetry, as some people would sooner cut off their left toe than read her inner ramblings when all they were after was some fantasy smex.

Arielle loves animals, tattoos, music, laughing, and reading and you can usually catch her entertaining one of these things at any given time. When not writing, she can be found walking one of her many fur babies, people watching in the mall, or jamming out in her car. She lives in the beautiful state of Colorado with her fish and fur-babies.

Arielle hopes to touch a heart one day, and show someone else they're not alone. And maybe, if she's lucky, she'll find out she's not alone either.

Facebook—http://www.facebook.com/Arielle-Adams-1364438227016845/
Twitter— @AllanaKephart

This Soldier's Heart

C.L. Foster
A Soldier's Sunset
♥

CL is eclectic, geeky, positive, nature-loving and completely non-"normal" (just the way she likes to be). She has been a fan of literature since she was a small child and finally decided to take her dreams (both waking and sleeping!) and do something positive with them.

CL has lived all over the world and has a Bachelor's degree in Criminal Justice, minoring in Psychology and Forensics. Which means you don't want to cross her because she knows how and where to hide a body so it's never found! She proudly admits to hearing voices in her head, but at times, her characters' impromptu visits can be rude and annoying. Thankfully, she has adequate patience for their shenanigans and can out ninja them any day of the week.

Website— http://www.authorclfoster.com
Facebook— https://www.facebook.com/AuthorCLFoster
Amazon—http://www.amazon.com/C.L.-Foster/e/B00A5GV1OS/

This Soldier's Heart

E.R. Rada
A Soldier's Sunset
♥

  E.R. Rada is a NY native whose mind is in a constant battle with reality and fiction. He's been penning his tales while expressing his inner most demons and heartfelt wishes since he was able to rhyme.
  Poetry and fantasy are his weapons of choice as his inner-most wish to be a dragon-riding, sword-wielding warrior has yet to come to fruition. E.R. knows there is no time limit on greatness, so he continues to float on his constant state of flux; learning, growing, and improving as time goes on.
  E.R. is a battle worn soldier who will quickly compare apples and oranges, simply because he's told he can't. Never one to conform, he embraces his nerdy/geek tendencies and is well known for creating new and interesting ways to do things (see: stubborn/the hard way). In doing things his own way, he has earned his way through life with plenty of battle scars, knowledge, and memories.

Goodreads—
https://www.goodreads.com/author/show/7045026.E_R_Rada

Lissa Lynn Thomas
Shut Up and Kiss Me
♥

Wife. Sister. Aunt. Author. Hopeless romantic. Netflix Binge Watcher. Music Lover.

Facebook - https://www.facebook.com/LissaLynnThomas.Author/

Twitter- https://twitter.com/lissalynnthomas

Pinterest- https://www.pinterest.com/lissalynnthomas

This Soldier's Heart

Made in the USA
Lexington, KY
06 July 2018